T0161955

CRIMSON VENGEANCE

By the Author

Necuratul

Necuratul 2: Rasputin's Rage

Necuratul 3: Blood Secrets

Salem's Fire

Bridge of Souls

Souls of Sorrow

Dirty Deeds

Crimson Vengeance

CRIMSON VENGEANCE

by

Sheri Lewis Wohl

2011

ISBN 10: 1-60282-539-4
ISBN 13: 978-1-60282-539-0

This Trade Paperback Original Is Published By
Bold Strokes Books, Inc.
P.O. Box 249
Valley Falls, NY 12185

First Edition: April 2011

CREDITS
EDITOR: SHELLEY THRASHER
PRODUCTION DESIGN: SUSAN RAMUNDO
COVER DESIGN BY SHERI (GRAPHICARTIST2020@HOTMAIL.COM)

For my grandmother,
Ilah Alvertta Wilson,
who by example taught me the beauty
of an open mind, an open heart,
and unconditional love.

PROLOGUE

London, 1522

Meriel floated into the room and Catherine's heart fluttered. Lady Meriel Danson was tall enough to meet the gaze of most of the men, with full breasts and eyes as green as emeralds. Her golden hair fell across her shoulders in lush curls and the crimson velvet dress flowed as she walked, her pale, flawless skin beautiful. She was the most stunning woman in the room and Catherine wasn't the only one who noticed. Tonight, all eyes followed her.

Like the precious jewel she was, Meriel smiled and flirted with adoring gentlemen as she crossed the room. They vied for her attention, some subtly, some with unabashed boldness most unbecoming. No one wished to be left out. The men wanted her. The women envied her. Catherine just smiled. Little did they know, Meriel's heart was already taken by a love as secret as it was forbidden.

Tonight, as every night, their secret would stay buried. It was more important to be pretty. To be seen. To dance. Neither of the young women would disappoint their families or their suitors. Indeed, Catherine and Meriel danced and smiled until late into the night, when the stars sparkled like diamonds in a jet black sky and the air outside was filled with the heavy scent of smoke.

It seemed an eternity before they were at last alone in the elegant carriage summoned to take them back into the city and to the world that demanded their unquestioned obedience. For two blessed hours they'd be alone, with darkness as their friend and protector. No prying eyes to spy on them or men with sweaty hands guiding them to the dance floor where they could subtly brush against their breasts and pretend it was unintentional.

Meriel's body pressed against Catherine's and everything else drifted away. Outside, the winter wind slapped against the carriage, the night sky a pitch black cover sprinkled with the twinkling light of a thousand stars. The wheels of the carriage bumped along the rutted and muddy road, but inside the carriage cushions were soft.

It was their time, their special world. Catherine lifted her arms to pull her precious love close. She kissed Meriel, her tongue darting between her lips, exploring, tasting. A fire began in Catherine's body, racing through her like the most powerful conflagration. How she treasured every moment, every kiss, every touch.

Meriel moaned and gathered her close as her hands moved to unlace the bodice of Catherine's fine wool dress. The supple fabric parted and her breast was bared, eager for the touch of Meriel's lips. Catherine sighed when Meriel took a nipple into her moist, hot mouth.

Catherine needed to feel the softness of Meriel's breasts and she pushed the velvet dress off Meriel's shoulders until she held them in her hands, brushing her thumbs across each nipple. She pinched them and smiled when Meriel groaned. In the darkness, they touched each other, skin to skin.

They made love inside the small black carriage as the storm outside rumbled and growled, growing ever louder as it raged. Catherine took no notice of the storm, her body alive with wondrous sensations. She cried out as Meriel's tongue brought her to a roaring climax.

She didn't want the night to end. How glorious it would be to stay here wrapped in Meriel's arms. Alas, too soon they would reach the city and once again become proper ladies to be dressed up like perfect little dolls. Their families expected obedience, if not enthusiasm, for events such as tonight's ball, all for the purpose of securing the highest bidders. Their fathers would sell them off in the name of socially acceptable marriages. In reality it was little different than the sale of prized livestock.

Catherine wouldn't be surprised to discover the deal for her own hand in marriage had already been made. Her father would like nothing better than to send her to the home of some rich and titled old man. Since the day of her mother's death one year earlier, it was as if her father could no longer stand the sight of her. Catherine would not think of that now. In this moment, she could share her love and her body with the one person who made her feel alive.

Catherine drifted into sleep despite the bumps and sways of the carriage. Her body was sated and her heart soaring. She rested her head against Meriel's velvet-covered shoulder and floated dreamily on the scent of jasmine perfume. She loved that smell.

Sometime later, Catherine awoke with a start. Disoriented, she slowly remembered where she was. She straightened and peered into the darkness of the empty carriage. Could they be home already? Her heart sank. The trip was too quick and she'd wasted so much of her time with Meriel asleep.

Catherine tidied her gown, patted her hair, and pulled the thick black cloak tight around her body. She opened the small door, stepped outside, and faltered, nearly losing her footing in the thick mud of the road. In the air wafted a hint of jasmine, but now it was mixed with something else: bitter, rancid. Catherine pulled her cloak tighter.

Silence hung oddly in the air, broken only by the soft snorts of horses nervously pawing the ground. Catherine turned her head, letting her gaze drift from the night sky to the landscape surrounding the stalled carriage. She pushed her hand against her lips at the same time a gust of wind ripped through the air, sending a spray of icy rain to slash across her face.

Their driver lay sprawled in the middle of the muddy road, his eyes sightless. Blood trickled from the wound that had almost separated his head from his body. Catherine spun away from the sight, her heart pounding.

As she stumbled from the carriage, her gaze was drawn to the sodden earth and what should not have been. Meriel lay in a pool of moonlight, dark streaks marring her perfect, white skin like shattered red silk tossed across a snow-covered meadow. Raindrops fell onto Meriel's pale cheeks. Mixed with the rain, blood slid down her face and neck, pooling on the ground beneath her tangled golden hair. Her head lay at an odd angle, and when Catherine realized why, her screams echoed through the darkness.

They can conquer
who believe
they can.

Virgil
70 BC–19 BC

CHAPTER ONE

Moses Lake, Washington
Present Day

Early spring usually arrived with blooming daffodils. This year it arrived with dead bodies. After all these years, Coroner Ivy Hernandez would have thought she'd be accustomed to death. She'd been at this game a long time and had seen everything from car accidents to suicides to drive-by shootings. Lately, a lot of drive-by shootings—thank you, twenty-first-century culture. Still, experience didn't make it any easier. Death was ugly, period.

With her hands stuck in the pockets of her light jacket, Ivy watched a deputy fish the latest unfortunate out of the drink. The lake was still cold as an iceberg, and no one had wanted that particular job.

The water, though clean compared to most in the country, was murky and didn't give up its secrets willingly. They'd found this guy, like the last one, only because the motion of the water pushed him toward the shore and a watchful neighbor had seen him bobbing in shallow water. Today, the morning air had a bite to it and the sky hung gray with a hint of moisture. If they were lucky they'd get the body loaded before the rain hit.

Dressed in a black wetsuit from neck to ankles, Deputy Daryl Wilson looked like something out of a horror movie as he waded in from the waist-deep water, pulling the body behind him. He was huffing and puffing by the time he had the dead man on dry land.

Sodden slacks stuck to long legs, and what was once a nice jacket hung on one arm, misshapen and ruined. A cotton dress shirt, open almost to the waist, had fallen back to reveal a smooth chest and a pale expanse of neck. His face held no expression, his eyes a pale, red-rimmed blue. Two puncture wounds at the base of his neck looked a bit like he'd lost the battle with a really big rattlesnake. It wasn't the wounds that made Ivy's heart race, or the blue of his eyes; it was the touch of color in his cheeks.

Ivy crouched and very gently touched the base of his neck. Icy flesh met her warm fingertips. Not even a whisper of a pulse. He was dead all right. Dead with just an ever-so-faint touch of pink in his cheeks.

"Shit," she muttered as she stood and pulled her cell phone from her pocket. Putting some distance between herself and the body, she turned her back to Daryl and the rest of the first responders who surrounded the inert form. "Riah," she said, after she heard the beep that put her into Riah's voice mail. "It's Ivy. I've got another one and I'll be heading your way late this afternoon. Give me a call as soon as you can."

Ivy flipped the phone shut, stuffed it into her pocket, and turned once more to face the dead man. It would be hours before she heard back from Riah. No problem. She didn't need confirmation on the cause of death. No, she needed a different kind of help from her old and trusted friend.

Daryl looked up from where he knelt next to the body. "Hey, Ivy, looks like we got us another one."

He tipped the dead man's head to the side revealing, for all of them to see, small raised punctures marring the expanse of white neck. The lake had stripped away any traces of blood from the wounds. Not that there would be any. There never was.

"Yes." Frowning, she stepped back to allow the newly arrived EMT to do his part. That took all of about thirty seconds, and then she received custody of the body.

Ivy went through the motions. She made notes and diagrams, photographed the body and the landing from every possible angle. Collected potential evidence, checked the body for personal property, and found nothing. No surprise there either.

By the time she finished, her cheeks were raw from the chill wind coming off the lake. Though the day was no longer young, the sky above was about the same as when they'd arrived. Gray and overcast seemed to be the agenda for today. If not for the latex gloves she now peeled off and stuffed into her pocket, her hands would be as cold as her face.

The deputies loaded the body, secure in the labeled and initialed black bag, into the back of her van. Certain things had to be done, both inside the guidelines and out. Time, at least for the moment, was on her side.

Despite the futility of the effort, Ivy walked through the typical steps for a homicide. She had to maintain appearances, after all. Grant County wasn't accustomed to this kind of evil, or even aware of it. If Ivy had her way, it never would be. Some things were best left unexplained. Let the fine folks of the county worry about gangbangers, drugs, and teenage violence. In other words, the regular stuff. She'd take care of the preternatural.

Ivy was the last to leave the park where the boat launch was now empty of both the living and the dead. For a long minute, she sat behind the wheel of the van and looked out over the park. Such a lovely place with trees and the gentle waves of the lake lapping against the swaying dock. It wouldn't be long before recreational boaters and the happy sounds of children playing on the beach filled the air. Every year a few lost their lives, yet the unmarred beauty of the natural setting still brought visitors who didn't fear the power of the water to take away life.

This was different. The man in the back of her van wasn't a drunken sportsman who fell out of his boat. He wasn't a recreational boater out for an evening cruise on the lake. No, more than likely this man's only sin was to be in the wrong place at the wrong time. He was a victim of pure circumstance, a lamb picked for the slaughter.

And he wasn't the first one.

Each time she hoped it was the last. Until recently, the victims she'd seen were in other places. At least here in Moses Lake, she really thought she'd be out of the loop. These types of victims were most often culled from the ranks of the large cities. In Washington, it was cities like Seattle, Tacoma, or Spokane. Moses Lake was too small and intimate to draw interest. Low and flat, the desert-like landscape didn't beckon to those who needed to hide. It was a place where too many questions would be asked.

When the first victim surfaced, Ivy speculated it was pure chance. A night creature passing through that would continue to bigger and greener fields. She handled the death with as much speed and diplomacy as she could. Questions were kept to a minimum, the press held off, and people quickly forgot the unusual demise of a troubled young man from an equally troubled family.

It was different now. One death could be an accident. Two was deliberate. It wasn't a fluke, and her town was no longer safe.

As Ivy pulled in at the rear of the coroner's office, she turned in her seat, looked over her shoulder, and backed the van up to the double doors. She didn't wait for anyone to come and help her unload. Instead, she opened the van's rear doors and slid the gurney out. She pushed it into the building and down the hall. Once through another set of double doors, she stopped and pulled a set of keys from her pocket. Ten years ago it never would have occurred to her to lock the cold room.

❖

Colin Jamison waited behind a clump of bushes for hours until what he'd swear was the entire Moses Lake police department and emergency-response personnel left the park. Once the van, the cruisers, and emergency vehicles drove away, he walked down to the boat launch. It was quiet now and he narrowed his eyes as he studied the deserted park. Why did he feel like he was very late for a grim game that started without him?

A blast of icy wind hit, and he stuffed his hands into his jacket pockets. He was tired, cold, and, most of all, cranky. He hated this town smack in the middle of the state of Washington. No Pacific Ocean here. No soaring mountains or endless forests. Here, there were too many tumbleweeds, too much sagebrush, and not enough trees. Not to mention way too many dead bodies with twin holes in the carotid. He'd be relieved when he'd completed the final task and could go home. He kept reminding himself how close he was and how soon it would all be over.

Now, if he could figure out this latest wrinkle.

Standing on the end of the gently swaying dock, Colin did a three-sixty. Not much to see. On the far shore, expensive homes spilled down to the edge of the water, their state-of-the-art docks bobbing slightly. On either side, water stretched as far as he could see. A few ducks paddled about, oblivious to the chilly water temperature.

Behind him were acres of park flowing down to the lake where groomed beaches awaited the sunshine-loving crowds. This early in the year the park was empty. It was, he had to admit, a good place to dump a body in the middle of the night.

With his eyes closed, Colin breathed deeply and listened. He hoped something would come to him—a scent, a sound—anything that might bring him closer to a killer. Nothing. He opened his eyes and pushed the hair off his forehead.

Like the last dump site, this one seemed to be little more than a convenient location. Right off I-90, it would be an easy on and off the interstate. Suck a little blood, drop a body in the lake, and be back on the road in a matter of minutes. Quick and easy for a bloodsucking creature on the move.

He left the beach behind and walked to where his car was parked in a nearby neighborhood. Fortunately no one seemed to have taken notice of or cared that he'd been parked there for a few hours. Once inside, Colin pulled a map from the black duffel on the backseat. The map spread out, he used a pen from the console to make a red X where the body was found. The circle was growing smaller as it moved in the direction of what Colin felt certain was the apex.

A little over a hundred miles to the east was the city of Spokane, and it was there the vampire appeared to be heading. Colin would be right behind her before the sun set.

It was five o'clock by the time he'd stopped for something to eat and then revisited the other drop sites for one last look around. He kept hoping something would come to him but it didn't. He still wasn't sure why this place. The day didn't have enough hours left to figure it out either.

Colin got back into his car and, after checking his navigator, had the address of the coroner's office in the center of the town. He put the car in gear and started to drive away from the park. He'd need to get into the place before dark to make sure the locals didn't get a nasty surprise.

Just a few blocks down Stratford Road, he made a U-turn to head back in the direction of the freeway. He almost missed it, then caught it out of the corner of his eye—the coroner's van heading south toward the on-ramp of I-90. When he closed the gap, he could see the driver was the same woman who'd been down on the dock earlier. The same one who secured the body bag. The van pulled onto the freeway headed east. He followed, keeping enough distance between the van and his car to avoid arousing suspicion. Not easy, considering the driver of the van wasn't exactly keeping to the speed limit. Getting pulled over wouldn't be good. It also wouldn't be good if he lost sight of the van. He pressed the accelerator.

"Slow down, will ya," he muttered.

There was always a chance the body from the lake was back at the morgue in Moses Lake and he was now in the process of chasing his tail, although he really didn't think so. His gut told him the two things he sought were right in front of him: one, in the back of the van, and the other, somewhere in the heart of the city ahead. He kept his speed up and the van in sight.

Colin yawned and rubbed his eyes with the back of one hand. Man, he was tired, and much more than just physically. His neck ached, his eyes burned, and his arms were leaden.

His spirit was weary as well. He was tired…mind, heart, and soul weary. The journey had been long and, thank God, was now about done. Truthfully, he'd be both relieved and lost. His entire life had been about the hunt, but what would he do once he completed it? He didn't have the answer. He wasn't sure how to live in a normal world where creatures that hunted in the night didn't exist. His reality was shrouded in mist and mystery, blood and fangs, death and undeath. It was almost impossible to even try to remember what life was like before.

It didn't matter. He'd worry about it later. First, he needed to finish what he'd started when barely in his teens. It was all he really knew how to do anyway. So, he kept his eyes on the van ahead and followed it toward the mountains, the pine trees, and the mighty Spokane River.

❖

Folk legends were simply that: legends. They had little to do with reality. Or, so most people wanted to believe. Doctor Riah Preston was both a folk legend and a reality. She was a creature of the night and over five hundred years old.

Riah was a vampire.

She didn't like it—not that she'd had a choice. She was turned without so much as a word on a gray, foggy winter night many centuries ago, just as she was offered under a veil of secrecy to satisfy a gambling debt when she was a newborn. Life had never given her choices, and it didn't give her one now. That was the one constant in her life.

Ivy's call today wasn't completely unexpected. For some time now she'd feared that more would come to leave their discarded victims like trash throughout the county. She could almost hear the whispers on the night air, the sounds of discontent in the fabric of her reality.

And, there were the calls from those who were not part of the darkness but were touched by it nonetheless. People with knowledge they should never have needed to possess, like Ivy Hernandez. It hurt that innocents, like Ivy, got drawn into her shadowy world. It just couldn't be helped. If there was another way, she'd be the first to grab it.

The darkness clouding this world for thousands of years was growing thin and weak, and not by accident. It was past time for change. Together, Riah and friends like Ivy worked to destroy the darkness until, one day, it would be Riah's turn to find the light. They would banish the darkness forever.

It would be easy to take the coward's way out. To simply lie down and allow a hunter to pierce her tired heart. Her life was lonely and, many times, like now, she wondered why she kept going. Nothing had been the same since the death of her beloved. Not her life, not her heart, not her very existence. The ache in her heart never seemed to go away and she grew tired of the pain. She longed for the peace a simple wooden stake could bring her.

People had a tendency to throw around terms like *soul mate* as easily as they tossed back cans of soda. They didn't really know what it meant. Only those whose lives became eternal could truly understand. Only those of that dark good-night fully grasped the complete meaning. True love, the kind that consumes the very soul, comes once, and when it's gone, that's it.

For Riah, it had been gone a very long time.

She shook her head and walked to her desk. *Enough with the soul searching and self-pity.* It was a waste of time because it changed nothing. She was alone and would be for eternity. This was her destiny. She'd earned it and she'd live it. The best she could do was try to make amends.

When Ivy's van pulled into the driveway, Riah hit the button to automatically open the doors to the loading dock. The sun was almost down and time was at a premium. They needed to move fast or their problems would multiply quickly.

Riah was an old vampire and, contrary to the legends, didn't go up in a puff of smoke when daylight touched her skin. While it was true she preferred the shadows night afforded, she could move in the light if need be. It was uncomfortable but far from deadly. Riah didn't race against the clock, but what awaited them in the back of Ivy's van did.

Jumping out of the open driver's side door, Ivy came around to the back of the van. She was a bit taller than Riah, maybe five feet five or so, with thick black hair that curled around a beautiful face. Ivy reminded Riah more of a favorite Spanish teacher than an investigator who dealt with death daily. She'd trained under Riah before taking the head job in her hometown of Moses Lake. Without a doubt, Ivy had been one of her best and brightest students. She was a natural and Riah always felt Ivy could go anywhere. Over the years they became much more than friends.

"Hola, chica," Ivy said as she threw open the rear doors of the van. "We best get on this guy pronto. He started twitching just about the time I hit the Maple Street Bridge. We're wasting moonlight, sister."

"Everything's ready and Adriana's on her way." Riah eyed the black bag. It was still and smooth. Contrary to Ivy's proclamation, nothing twitched now.

"Bueno." Ivy snapped the doors of the van shut and pushed the gurney to the double doors Riah held open. The wheels squeaked softly as it rolled down the brightly lit hallway.

The slight rustle of movement inside the black bag made Riah glance back at the gurney. "Damn," she muttered as she hurried ahead of Ivy down toward the autopsy suite.

"I told you," Ivy said. "He's a feisty one. Never would have guessed it from the boring business suit he was wearing when we pulled him out of the lake."

Inside the morgue, Riah moved fast. The window in which to do her work was small, and seconds were ticking away in what seemed like double-time.

CHAPTER TWO

Ivy stood next to Riah and they both stared at the body on the stainless-steel autopsy table. She should concentrate solely on the victim, yet Riah's hands caught her attention. They always did. They were beautiful, and it amazed her how they could be so lovely after centuries.

Though she knew the truth about her friend's life, the reality of it still gave her pause. How many years had she and Riah known each other? Fourteen? Fifteen? In that time, Ivy had changed from an energetic college intern with a fresh face and long dark hair, to a mature woman with tiny lines around her eyes and strands of white peppering her now-short hair. The first time she stood next to Riah beside an autopsy table, she was an eager student. Now they stood side-by-side as seasoned contemporaries. Ivy felt every one of those fifteen years and suspected she looked them as well.

Riah, on the other hand, appeared as vital and attractive as the first day Ivy met her. Her auburn hair was still long and shiny with just a hint of wave. Not a single line distracted from her intelligent hazel eyes. At just a touch over five feet, she was thin, athletic, and very pretty. She didn't look more than twenty-one, though once she opened her mouth, no one would mistake her for young or inexperienced. Maturity and knowledge radiated from Riah despite her youthful appearance and diminutive size.

A door opened behind them, the sound little more than a swish. Ivy turned in time to see Adriana James step through. Like Riah, she was a small woman, though Adriana sported far more curves than Riah. Her black hair was cut short and close to her head, her black eyes full of life. Ivy liked Adriana quite a lot. She was smart, educated, and determined. If anyone could find what they searched for, it was Adriana James.

She was also in love with Riah, though Ivy didn't think Riah even noticed. Not that it had happened overnight. The three of them had been working side-by-side for the better part of a decade, and Ivy had seen the change occur slowly, steadily. It wasn't that Adriana was blatant about her feelings for Riah. No, she was far more subtle. A look here. A soft touch there. A sigh when she thought no one was looking.

It occurred to Ivy as she watched Adriana bring her case to the table, in all the time she'd known Riah, she'd never been involved with anyone, man or woman. At least as far as Ivy knew. Sad if it was true. She didn't wish that kind of loneliness on anyone.

Then again, once Riah had shared her secret with Ivy it explained so much. Of course she looked young—she hadn't aged since she was attacked five centuries earlier. Truthfully, it had taken awhile to fully grasp that her teacher and friend was a vampire.

Vampires were fiction, not reality, or so she believed until a decade ago. Once she finally got it, she was intrigued. She hit Riah with at least a million questions. Some she answered, some she didn't. Ivy soon learned certain topics were off-limits, like Riah's family, her love life, and how she was turned. Definitely how she was turned. It was the only time Ivy ever felt the full force of Riah's fury. She didn't want to again.

"What have we got?" Adriana's voice broke into her thoughts.

"Same as the last one," Ivy explained. "Found him floating in my lake."

"Wicked," Adriana murmured.

Ivy and Adriana both jumped when the body on the table twitched, legs quivering and fingers splaying. Riah didn't even blink.

"Ladies," Riah said like a teacher in front of a daydreaming classroom. "We're running out of time. We need to get to work."

She was right. Riah's words propelled them into action. Ivy pulled four pair of handcuffs from her jacket pocket and attached one each to eyebolts at the corners of the table—not exactly the standard-issue autopsy table. Then she attached a cuff from each to the body's arms and legs.

At the same time Ivy was securing lake-man to the table, Adriana opened her case. She pulled vials and a large syringe from inside and proceeded to snap one vial into the syringe. The first blood sample she drew was from the neck wound. When the vial was full of deep crimson blood, she removed it and popped in a second vial. The next sample came from his right arm, the third from his left.

Adriana was putting everything into her case when, with eyes wide open, the body on the table strained against the handcuffs. An inhuman roar tore from his throat, bouncing off the walls of the cold room. The sound sent Ivy's blood pressure sky-high. It didn't matter how many times she'd seen this in the last ten years; it still scared the bejesus out of her. It was nothing like depicted in movies or books. It was so much worse. She jumped away from the table just as Riah moved in with a wooden stake in one hand and a heavy mallet in the other. Ivy turned away as another piercing scream made her shudder.

Then, nothing but silence filled the room.

"Damn it." Colin quickened his step along the side of the building. Why couldn't these buildings have more than one set of doors? He'd had no trouble scaling the security fence, but gaining entrance to the building so far proved to be more problematic. The doors were locked up nice and secure with mag-card readers that he'd learned from long experience were hard to circumvent. He kept looking. There had to be a way in.

A few minutes earlier he watched the two women roll a body into the building through the rear doors. It didn't take a huge leap to figure out the body was the same one pulled from the chilly waters of Moses Lake, though none of it made much sense. Why bring a body some hundred-plus miles from the county of the murder? And when there were facilities for autopsy in the same county? One sure way to get the real story —only first he needed to figure out how to get in the damn place.

A muffled scream came from somewhere deep within the building. He stopped in his tracks. *Ah, shit.* All hell was about to break loose and he was the only one who could stop it. He moved even faster along the perimeter of the facility. Finally, he saw it. Colin slammed his hand against a round red button and waited. He tapped his foot and drummed his fingers on top of the red button, ready to smack it again if need be.

It seemed to take forever before a gray-uniformed, beefy-armed rent-a-cop opened the door. He filled the doorway like a block of concrete and effectively blocked Colin's entrance—but Colin wasn't intimidated. This bozo was an obvious wannabe who'd never be. He just didn't know it yet.

"The ME's office is closed. You'll need to come back tomorrow." He popped his gum and rested a hand on his baton. His face was neutral though his eyes sparked. Probably practiced the look in the mirror every night.

Colin narrowed his own eyes. "Not acceptable."

He threw a carefully placed punch to the man's neck and the guy went down like a big bag of wet sand. Colin stepped over him before pulling him inside. A second scream, louder now that he was inside, echoed through the hallway. Leaving the unconscious man on the floor, he ran in the direction of it.

The whole time he was sprinting through the empty hallway, he kept thinking something wasn't right. Then it hit him: after the second scream…nothing. It didn't make sense, there should be more noise. The thing would be disoriented and hungry and looking for a way out. These things could get more than a little vocal when first rising. So where was the noise? *Please, Jesus, let me be in time.*

Colin continued to run down the hallway, pushing open doors as he went. One on his right. Two on his left. Where was he?

Goddamnit, he had to find him. Everyone here would die if he didn't get to this creature now.

At the end of the long hallway, he smacked a wide door with his palm. It flew open, banging against a wall with a deafening crash, and he stopped, sliding on the smooth tile. The door hit his shoulder as it swung back. Bright light filled the room, spilling down like a halo around three women who stood by an occupied autopsy table. They looked up in unison, surprise mirrored on all three faces.

"May I help you?" This came from the smallest woman.

Young and pretty, she had a voice filled with authority. Had to be a tech of some sort. He didn't need a flunky, he needed the boss.

"I'm looking for the ME." He peered around the room.

"That would be me. I'm Dr. Preston and you are?" Her eyes seemed to bore through him.

"In a hurry." Colin didn't have time for the young woman's games. He needed the ME and he needed him now. Her dark, menacing look didn't cut it with him. Quite the opposite, in fact. This youngster was wasting his time.

"And I'm in the middle of an autopsy." A single eyebrow rose though her voice did not.

He paused and studied her. "You can't be the ME." So maybe she wasn't a tech. Med student, maybe?

"I can and I am. Now, sir, as I said, I'm rather busy at the moment." Ice began to drip from her words.

His gaze went to the table and his mouth opened. Nothing came out. It couldn't be. Less than five minutes ago, he'd heard the scream. The man, the one pulled from Moses Lake, had turned. Colin would bet his life on it. Yet the same man was on the table and opened up like a treasure chest with a very precise Y-incision. He was, as the old saying went, dead as a doornail, and an ME who looked to be about twelve years old glared at Colin like the intruder he was.

None of this made the least bit of sense. Not the dead man. Not the young woman who declared she was, in fact, the ME for Spokane County. "I…I…ah…"

"Well, that certainly clears things up."

She slowly laid an instrument on the table. It made a slight ping as metal met metal. Inside the quiet room, the sound was like a cannon shot. Her gaze came up to his face, her eyes dark and intelligent. The face might be that of an adolescent, the eyes were not.

"I think," he began to back toward the door he'd come through only minutes before. "I think, I've possibly made a mistake."

The woman's eyes narrowed. "Who are you?"

"My mistake." He turned and ran.

Colin was in his car with the engine running in less than a minute. One thing this job had taught him was speed. He knew when to get out of Dodge. He didn't look back as he sped away from the offices of the Spokane County Medical Examiner.

At the hotel, he booked a room with a balcony overlooking Riverfront Park. The downtown jewel was once the site of dirty rail yards, renovated in 1974 for the Spokane World's Fair. Or so the helpful desk clerk informed him. It was impressive, even to his tired mind. He couldn't envision what it might have looked like years ago riddled with train tracks, rail riders, and boxcars. These days, in addition to the lush lawns, paved walking paths, and an incredible historic carrousel, the river ran right through the middle of the park, the waters deep and clear. It was all so beautiful. If only evil didn't lurk beneath everything majestic and beautiful.

He took off his jacket, unloaded his weapons, and dropped to the bed. God, he was tired. Eyes closed, he prayed for rest, except sleep wouldn't come. Instead, he pondered what he'd seen and it still didn't make sense.

Darkness had fallen well before he'd done the smack-down on the security guard. With darkness would come the man's transformation into the preternatural realm of monsters. Short of a stake through the heart, he would have become a vampire—not a body laid out for autopsy.

Unless…

Colin jumped up off the bed and headed to the shower, peeling off clothes as he went. He was naked and alert by the time he stepped beneath the spray. The water was cool and refreshing. His mind cleared instantly. Weariness vanished as if the water washed it down the drain.

"I'll be a son of a bitch." He slapped the wall, making water spray into his eyes. The sting made him blink.

He pictured the three women in the autopsy room: the tiny ME with the intense eyes; the beautiful Hispanic coroner he'd followed from Moses Lake; and the third, a petite and attractive black woman, who stood nervously in the background with a specimen case held tight in her hands. To the casual observer, they were simply three professional women performing the business of death, just doing their jobs.

He shook his head and propped both hands against the tile. Fresh water flowed down his back, cooling his skin and clearing his mind more fully as he whispered, "They knew."

CHAPTER THREE

R iah had an uneasy feeling about their intruder. She became even more uneasy when she found Brett, the evening security guard, in a crumpled heap just inside the rear door to the facility. The good news was Brett was still alive. The bad news... he was a big guy, and to take him down without a sound was an impressive feat. Nope, not good at all.

She couldn't have been more than a few seconds behind the stranger and yet he'd slipped out of the building so fast, she'd lost sight of him. Riah still held an advantage. He was human and she wasn't. No matter how fast he was, she was faster. If she had time, she could track him and find out exactly who he was.

Except she didn't have time. Not right now anyway. She shut the door and waited to hear the click of the lock. One uninvited intruder a night was plenty. No one else was going to get through the door unless she let them in, although she wasn't totally convinced the locked door would have stopped the last visitor even if Brett hadn't opened it for him.

Why? Why would the man be so intent on coming into her facility he would risk not just the security guard but the cameras as well? She intended to find out. Riah checked Brett's pulse, found it strong and steady. Before she headed back to the autopsy room, she placed a call to the Spokane police. As much as she'd like to keep this incident quiet, that wasn't possible. The minute Brett became involved, it slipped out of her control. Because the morgue was located in the same complex as the police department, it took only a few minutes for an officer to arrive. As soon as she could make a graceful exit, she returned to Ivy.

"Who was that guy?" Ivy had her head down, her hands busy over the body on the table.

"I don't know."

Ivy looked up at Riah then, her dark eyes hazy behind the shield of her headgear. Dressed in green scrubs, her hair covered by a cap and her gloved hands slightly bloody, she looked a bit like she'd just stepped out of a horror movie. Though, in reality, it *was* horror. Certainly the path she and Ivy chose was macabre to some. It was the dirty business of death most people preferred not to think about.

It was more about life than death for Riah. She'd been undead a very long time and needed to understand why. What took her youth and turned her into something she hated to think about? She knew who it was, or perhaps more accurately what it was, that took her life on a dark winter night. She'd never forget him or how he'd looked when she destroyed him. There was a lot to be said about the teachings in the Old Testament—an eye for an eye.

Now she searched for something more concrete though elusive. She wanted to know *what* set her apart from Ivy and from Adriana. If she could discover that secret, perhaps she could find the key to her own salvation. No more blood, no more immortality, no more secrets.

Beneath the light green cap, Ivy's brow wrinkled. "Odd," she said as she stared down at the body.

Riah let out a breath and pulled a cap over her hair and a shield over her face. None of the blood or fluids encountered would harm her; she had just formed the habit during her many years of pretending to be human.

"What's odd?" she asked Ivy when she once again stood at the table's edge.

"Oh, I don't know," Ivy muttered. "We should see some sign of a struggle, but there's nothing." She picked up one of his hands and showed his smooth palm to Riah. "It's like this guy let the vamp kill him. At least the last victim tried to fight. Why wouldn't he put up a fight?"

The unmarred skin didn't surprise her. It was so easy to lure a willing victim, though not one of the secrets of her past she'd shared with Ivy. She wasn't about to now either. Instead she said, "Let's see what this guy can tell us." She moved to the other side of the table.

"Hey." Adriana spoke from behind Ivy. "I'm going to my lab. I'll call you later." Adriana touched Riah lightly on the shoulder as she passed. Her fingers were warm even through the protective garment.

Riah nodded and forced her focus to the body. Adriana had plenty to do with her samples, and she needed to do her work here.

On the table, his chest was opened, the heart exposed. The damage that the small wooden spike had inflicted was clearly evident under the harsh fluorescent lights. "We'll need to camouflage that." Riah pointed to the ragged edges of the hole caused by the stake.

"You got it," Ivy said, and picked up a scalpel to begin the work of making this body appear to be a run-of-the-mill homicide victim.

The autopsy was completed, notes made, and the victim once more secured in the back of Ivy's van and on his way back to Moses Lake by a little past ten. Riah shrugged out of her bloody scrubs, washed up, then slipped on a soft leather jacket. She turned out the lights in the autopsy suite and walked down the hall.

Brett was busy in the main control room making his report to the uniformed police officer, and while she'd also been questioned about the intruder, she'd successfully pled ignorance. She should have told everyone about the tall stranger who barged into the autopsy room. She could have given a very accurate description. That she didn't wasn't only out of character, it was potentially dangerous. She didn't choose to explore her reasons too deeply.

In her car, Riah reached into a cooler and pulled out a small, thick plastic bag. She sighed and accepted the inevitable. She needed the blood, and if she didn't take it this way, her cravings would rule her. If she allowed that to happen…well, she didn't want to think about how it would end.

She started the car and turned the heat on high. For a few minutes, she let the container rest on top of the heater vent. Taking it from a bag was bad enough. Ice-cold from the cooler was unbearable. Even a vampire had her limits.

Once the blood was gone and she felt refreshed and sated, she turned the heat down, put the car in Drive, and pulled through the security gate onto the city street. She intended to go directly home. Instead, she found herself heading north. Ten minutes later, she pulled off Northwest Boulevard and into the driveway of a tidy one-story house along the ridge of the hill overlooking the river. Adriana's house. So much for good intentions.

For a long time, she sat in the car. Really, she should go home. Adriana would let her know tomorrow what, if anything, she'd learned. Except she didn't want to go home. Not tonight. It might have been the visit by the strange man that had her so disquieted now. Maybe. Maybe not.

In all honesty, she'd been unsettled lately, as if something in her life was amiss. Perhaps it was anxiety over not making ground on her search for a cure. Again—maybe. Maybe not.

It still didn't explain why she was sitting in Adriana's driveway like some kind of stalker. Or perhaps it did. It'd be stupid to pretend she didn't know Adriana was attracted to her. Christ almighty, she was over five hundred years old. She knew what attraction was when she saw it. She was also exceptionally good at deflecting it. Practice did make perfect after all.

Right now, she tried to tell herself she came to check on Adriana's progress with the samples collected earlier. If it meant she'd have to spend a little quality time in close proximity to Adriana, well, then… okay, but it was all business. It was about the cure.

What a crock. Even to her it sounded stupid. She wasn't fooling herself and it was a stretch to believe she could fool Adriana either.

For the first time in a very long time, Riah had the hots for a woman. And she had it bad. If she believed in love, she could almost convince herself she was falling in love with Adriana. Except her chance at love had died many, many centuries ago. This was simply lust.

She took a deep breath and swung the car door open. Riah would just go on in, ask Adriana what she'd found, and then go home. Yes, that's what she'd do. This *thing* she was feeling would pass once she took a few minutes to chat with Adriana about business.

At the front door, Riah pushed the doorbell. It would take Adriana a minute to get to the door if she was downstairs in the lab, and that was fine since it would give her another minute to compose herself. When the door swung open immediately, Riah wasn't sure what surprised her most: that Adriana was already at the door—or that she was naked.

❖

By the time Ivy got the body tucked back into the cooler, the door locked, and the report notes uploaded, it was past midnight. Everything was in place for a properly signed death certificate listing the official cause of death as homicide by knife attack. Sure, the entire team at the lake this morning noticed the puncture wounds on the man's neck. They'd even taken a dozen or so pictures to document the marks. That didn't mean she had to write it up as a vampire attack. Like folks would accept it as the truth anyway. People didn't believe preternatural creatures roamed somewhere between shadow and light. Even if they did, deep in their hearts they didn't want to. Ignorance was bliss.

The majority of cultures throughout the world had some version of a vampire. They were, for the most part, relegated to fiction and folklore. Ivy would be more than happy to leave them all there, except she couldn't. She wasn't particularly fond of the lessons she'd had to learn the last decade or so. It wasn't fair. She was going through her life ignorant and happy until the night Riah came to her with an incredible story. Sometimes having friends really sucked. Especially if one of those friends turned out to be a bona-fide bloody-fanged vampire, albeit a very pretty one with an IQ guaranteed to ensure an invitation to Mensa.

Ivy sank into the chair at her desk and ran a hand through her hair. Talk about tired. If it was up to her, she'd lay her head on the stack of file folders and sleep for a day or two. Alas, too much work to do and too many details to cover. Sleep would have to wait.

When her phone rang, she jumped. Her hand to her heart, she picked up the handset.

"Ivy Hernandez."

"Ivy, this is Phil from over at K-5 News."

"Hey, Phil." She kept her voice friendly even though, at this time of the night, chances were this wasn't a social call.

"So what's up with your floater? I've been trying to catch you all afternoon."

"Sorry, I've been out most of the day. I called in a little help from Spokane."

"Yeah, so I heard. Why?"

"Why what?" She was good at playing dumb when the situation called for it.

"Why did you call in help?"

"Look, Phil, there'll be an official release in the morning and you can read it all for yourself."

"Ah, come on, Ivy. It's your pal here. We started first grade together, remember? I carried your lunch. I was the big strong friend who pushed Joey Stevens when he tried to kiss you. So, here's the deal. I got the five a.m. news coming up with nothing to lead, and you could help me out."

The minute she heard his voice, she knew he'd try to play the old-pal card. Phil was actually pretty good at his job, and Ivy had wondered more than once what kept him here in Moses Lake. Even when they were back in high school, she always thought he'd move on to bigger, better things. So far, he was the home boy who stayed home and used every connection he could to get his story.

"I could, but I'm not. You know the drill, old pal. Come by after nine and you can pick up a copy of the official release."

"You're sure? Not even for an old and dear friend?"

"Not even for an old and dear friend. I like my job, Phil, and I'd like to keep it, if you catch my drift."

"Well, can't blame a guy for trying."

"Good night, Phil."

"Night, beautiful."

She hung up the phone, snapped off the light, and headed out the door. It was time to get out of the office before another reporter called. Didn't anybody sleep anymore?

Traffic was light and the night clear. Beautiful stars hung golden against the inky black sky. People could pick on Moses Lake all they wanted, but it could be a really lovely place. Especially on nights like tonight. The air was clear, the sky was magical, and, for the moment, things were peaceful.

As she was crossing the bridge, lights flickered off the lake waters. So postcard-picturesque. The pleasant feeling lasted too, at least until she pulled into her driveway. First another vampire, then Phil, now this. God definitely wasn't smiling on her today.

Ivy slammed the door of her car and then stomped toward the shiny black pickup parked at her curb. "I swear to God, Jorge, if I carried a gun I'd shoot your ass right here, right now."

Jorge Santos stepped out of the truck and smiled. His wavy black hair was pulled back in a ponytail, the way he was well aware that Ivy liked it best. In black jeans and a white shirt, opened at the neck, he was hot and knew it. On any other woman, his Hollywood good looks would work. Jorge's problem was, Ivy wasn't any woman. He was just about the last person on earth she wanted to see.

"Bonita," he drawled. "You would never hurt me."

"Try me. I wasn't kidding the first time I told you to stay away. Or the third. Or the fifth." She put a hand on his chest and pushed him toward the curb.

Jorge put his hand over hers, his fingers softly stroking her skin. "Feel my heart beat for you, bonita?"

Ivy snatched her hand away and took a step back. At the same time, she pulled her cell phone out of her pocket and held it up for him to see. "I'm giving you exactly thirty seconds to put your ass back in that truck and get out of here. If you don't, I'll call the sheriff. Did I ever mention I have him on speed dial?"

Jorge's face darkened and his eyes narrowed. "Are you seeing him? Are you sleeping around on me?"

Ivy struggled to hold back her fury. "Oh, for Christ's sake, Jorge. I'm not *yours,* and Sheriff Nevell is on my speed dial because he promised to throw your skinny brown butt in jail the next time you harassed me."

"Harass you?" Jorge threw his hands wide. "How can your husband harass you?"

"Ex-husband," she said, slow and loud.

Jorge crossed his arms over his chest and stared directly into her eyes. "I do not agree."

Ivy pointed a finger in his direction. "You have no choice. The decree has been signed, sealed, and delivered. Now give it up and go back to one of your *putas*."

She was surprised how little it hurt these days. Now instead of the stabbing pain in her heart at the mention of the women Jorge slept with, she felt weariness. Jorge was beautiful, and in bed, holy Moses, the man was incredible. Of course, if she'd given it some thought before she married him, she might have realized he was good because he'd had practice. Lots and lots of practice. Both before they were married and after. The after part, not necessarily all with Ivy either.

Ironically, he could never see the problem. To give Jorge credit, he truly believed in the concepts of love, honor, and cherish. Jorge also believed screwing every female on two legs in no way conflicted with his vow to love, honor, and cherish Ivy. The fact that Ivy did still seemed to astound him.

Truthfully, she'd moved on a while ago, and really, really wanted him to do the same. At least twice a week, or so it seemed, she'd find him on her doorstep. At first, seeing him was heart-wrenching. Then it became tiresome. Now, it was plain infuriating. Particularly considering that a vampire running around her county dropping bodies was taking up just about all her energy. She didn't need Jorge or his steadfast denial.

He stared at her for a long moment, then shrugged. "Pity, bonita, we are so good together."

"Were, Jorge. It's past tense, and the sooner you get that through your thick head, the happier we'll all be."

In the pickup, he leaned out the window and shook his head. "No, Ivy, you're wrong. I'll never be happier without you. *Te amo*."

Ivy met his eyes and her voice was rock steady as she said, *"Yo no te quiero."* She spun around and strode to the house. She didn't turn to look back when Jorge roared away, the big tires of the truck squealing on the asphalt.

❖

The shower helped, but Colin was still curious about the scene inside the medical examiner's office. It seemed like the thing to do now was relax and dig a little deeper to see what he could come up with. He started toward the desk and then changed his mind. One thing could help make a few hours of research easier. He zipped open his suitcase and pulled out a bottle of twelve-year-old scotch. Breaking the seal and unscrewing the top, he put his nose close to inhale the rich scent of the amber liquor. Nice.

With glass in hand, he sat at the small desk and powered up his laptop. Logged into the secure site, he searched. Nothing. He stared at the unhelpful screen. By all accounts, he should be the only hunter here. Then again, if the women knew the man pulled from Moses Lake would turn, it made sense that one of them would have to be a hunter. Except that scenario was impossible. He was the only one. So a couple of million-dollar questions remained: who were the women in that autopsy suite and what were they doing with the vampire's victim?

He tried some more search avenues and still came up with squat. Taking a long swallow of the scotch, he dug his cell phone out of the jeans he'd tossed on the bed. No sense screwing around, might as well go right to the top. It wouldn't be the first time he'd been left out of the loop, and if this was one of those times, he wanted to know.

The call was answered on the first ring, it always was. "Colin."

"Monsignor."

"Is there a problem?"

"That's what I'm calling to find out."

"Perhaps you should explain."

Colin did, in great detail. He finished by asking, "I was under the impression I was on this mission alone, am I mistaken?" The possibility that Monsignor would lie to him after all these years made him tense his shoulders and grind his teeth.

There was a long silence on the other end. "No, you are not."

His shoulders relaxed, a little. "Then who do you think these women are?"

"I do not know," the monsignor said on a sigh.

The phone still held to his ear, Colin walked onto the balcony and looked out over the river at the full moon. How many preternatural beings were out tonight? The moon huge and round was a call to the weres. And to the vampire he hunted.

"We need to know who they are."

"Agreed. I'll check with the council and call you with any additional information I discover."

"I don't like this, Monsignor. I don't have a good feeling about any of it."

"Neither do I."

"I'll be in touch tomorrow." He was just about to click off when the monsignor's voice stopped him.

"Colin?"

"Yes, sir."

"Be careful."

The two words sent a chill down his back. "Always."

CHAPTER FOUR

With effort, Riah found her voice. "I...I came by to see what you found with the blood samples." Adriana motioned for Riah to come into the house and so she did.

"Do you really want to talk about the results of the blood tests?" Adriana rested her back against the door, both hands on her hips. "Because, frankly, I don't."

"I don't understand." It was almost impossible to concentrate on anything except Adriana. She wasn't just beautiful, she was stunning.

A slow, sexy smile turned up the corners of Adriana's mouth. "It's simple. I like you. You like me. We can dance around it all we want, Riah, but the truth's right in front of us and has been for quite a while. I'm tired of the pretense."

She could argue and even sound convincing, except she wouldn't. Adriana wasn't the only one tired of pretending. "It's complicated." Riah shifted from one foot to the other and refused to meet her eyes.

"Not really. I'm human. You're a vampire. But, unless I'm mistaken, all the parts work the same."

"That's not what I mean." Riah rubbed a hand over her eyes.

Adriana stood very close. Her body a whisper away from Riah's. Her perfume sweet, alluring. "Then tell me what you mean." Adriana ran her tongue along her bottom lip.

Riah's fingers flexed. Adriana smelled like vanilla and woman. It made her want to run her hands down her dark, silky skin, across her lean hips and firm ass. To take one erect nipple into her mouth. It had been so very long.

She sighed and said, "I don't get involved with friends. Ever." It was never a good idea no matter how much she wanted to. She'd learned that lesson the hard way a long time ago.

"Why?" Adriana's voice was very matter-of-fact.

Why? "Friends are too hard to come by." That much of the truth was pretty cut and dried even if it wasn't all of it.

"And you're afraid if we become lovers it will end badly and we'll no longer be friends?"

Thank God she understood. "Yes."

"Bullshit."

Riah jerked. She thought Adriana got it and agreed. "I don't want to lose you as a friend," she insisted. She valued her friendship with Adriana more than she wanted to make love to her.

Adriana took one of Riah's hands and put it on her breast. Her skin was soft, hot. "You're afraid of something, Riah Preston, but it's not of losing me as a friend."

One part of her wanted to snatch her hand away. The other part couldn't, the feel of the full, lush breast making her breath come faster. "What do you want from me?" she rasped, and hated the way she sounded almost desperate.

"You know what I want and tonight we're done with pretending. I love you, Riah, and I want to make love to you. You don't have to love me back, I've enough for us both. Just don't deny me. I've waited a very long time for this."

Her mind screamed no. Her heart, yes. Her heart won. Riah put her free hand behind Adriana's head, pulled her close, and kissed her. She left her other hand on Adriana's breast, brushing her thumb over the erect nipple.

"I can't believe you answered the door naked," Riah said with a laugh when she came up for air. God, how wonderful Adriana tasted.

Adriana smiled and tilted her head to one side. Her eyes sparkled. "I saw your car in the driveway and decided it was now or never. I was out of my clothes in about ten seconds. You know the old saying, no guts, no glory."

Riah laughed and hugged her. "Silly girl."

"Horny girl, you mean." Adriana stepped back and winked.

She took Riah's hand and pulled her down a hallway. Riah didn't resist. In the big picture, a good idea would be to turn around and go home. She kept walking.

The door at the end of the hallway opened into a large tasteful bedroom. The bed was a big four-poster of rich mahogany covered with a deep red duvet and mounds of pillows. Adriana slid to the center of the bed and rested back against the pillows. Her body was gorgeous, with nice rounded hips and full breasts with dark nipples.

"Okay, vamp, let's see the goods."

"You're a bit bossy." Riah raised an eyebrow. This was a side of Adriana she'd never seen before. She liked it.

"Oh, I can be more than bossy. I can be downright domineering." Adriana licked her lips and smiled.

Riah smiled back. "I'm liking you better by the minute."

"Then strip."

So that's how it was going to be. A little wild, a little daring, and a whole lot exciting. The quiet ones were always full of surprises.

A buzz rippled through Riah's body and her fingers trembled as she slipped out of her shirt. Kicking off her shoes, she pushed jeans and panties down her legs. Cool air met her bare skin.

"Nice," Adriana murmured from the bed, one hand stroking the patch of black hair between her legs. "Let's see the rest."

Slowly, Riah unhooked the lacy black bra. It fell to the floor on top of the rest of her discarded clothing.

At the bed, she lowered herself next to Adriana. Again, she kissed Adriana, parting her lips with her tongue to push inside. She tasted sweet, which made her want more.

She explored Adriana's body, her skin hot. She reached between her legs, wanting to feel the wetness and the warmth there, but Adriana stopped her.

"Do you trust me?" Adriana asked against her lips, biting lightly but hard enough to draw just a hint of blood.

The metallic taste of blood sent a feverish rush throughout Riah's body. She shuddered but held tight to her control even as her fangs lengthened just a touch. She took a deep breath, and they receded.

Riah pulled away to study Adriana's face. She didn't have to think long for the answer. "Of course I do."

Very few people were privy to the secret of her life, and the fact that Adriana was one of them seemed, at least to Riah, to speak to the issue of trust. She was surprised Adriana even felt she needed to ask.

Adriana smiled and rolled away. Before Riah could protest, Adriana pulled four silken scarves from the bedside table. All were a beautiful shade of emerald. "Do you trust me?" she asked again, and waved the scarves over the bed.

For a moment Riah drew a blank, and then it hit her. Her entire body tingled. Talk about surprises. Adriana seemed full of them tonight.

"Yes," she answered on a sly smile.

She moved to the center of the bed. On her back, she settled her head against the pillows. She spread her legs and arms as if she was making a snow angel.

Adriana took the scarves and one by one tied her hands and feet to the four bedposts. Her touch was gentle as she wrapped each scarf around an ankle or a wrist. As she tied each hand, she kissed the palm. As she tied each ankle, she kissed the bottom of each foot. Riah's heart pounded like a drum at each feather-light touch of Adriana's lips. It was as close as she ever got to feeling alive again.

Once Riah was all tied up, Adriana moved back onto the bed to straddle her. She was wet, hot, and Riah pushed against her. The buzz became a roar.

"Patience, my love." Adriana kissed her, and this time she was the one who pushed her tongue in. "Your safe word is 'sunlight.'"

"Safe word," Riah whispered. Why would she need a safe word? If she wanted out of the restraints, she'd be free in less than a second. She was only lying here tied up because she chose to allow it.

As if reading her thoughts, Adriana said, "This is about pleasure, Riah, not power. If I do anything to you that isn't pleasurable, say the safe word and I'll stop. No questions asked." She ran her hand down Riah's cheek, her neck, and across her sensitive breasts.

Riah smiled. "Sounds perfect."

Adriana reached into the drawer of the nightstand once more, a breast brushing Riah's lips. When she straightened up, she held a black scarf in her hand. Where were all the scarves coming from?

Adriana held it in both hands and bent forward. This time, her erect nipple met Riah's mouth full on, and she sucked it greedily. As she did, Adriana gently tied the silky black scarf around her eyes, sending her into delicious darkness.

Jorge Santos left his wife's house even though he didn't like it. He didn't agree with Ivy at all. But, at times it was much better to retreat than to fight with her. Tonight was definitely one for retreat. Ivy was a woman of moods, and she was in one now. She was much more fun when she was relaxed and pliable. Of course, it had been a really long time since she'd been either. At least around him.

The parking lot at his favorite lounge was full when he pulled in. *Good.* He needed more than just a drink, and by the look of things, the field would be promising. It took two complete loops around the lot before he found a space for the truck.

He flipped down the visor and studied himself in the small lighted mirror. He smiled, ran a hand over his hair, and pushed the visor back up. He popped open the glove box and took out a small bottle of cologne, splashed a little in his hands, and patted his neck. He rolled his head before straightening his shirt. Now, he was ready.

Inside, a band played and the noise level was just this side of a roar. *Perfect.* Jorge sauntered into the lounge and could feel eyes on him as he crossed to the bar. His smile was his best feature. It drew women like flies.

He scanned the room at the same time he moved through it and quickly forgot his irritation at Ivy's rebuff. One woman's rejection was another woman's golden opportunity.

It might turn out to be a great night after all. He liked what he was seeing. "Promising" didn't begin to describe the crowd tonight, even given the late hour. He winked at a black-haired beauty in a skin-tight shirt that barely kept her boobs from falling out. *Un hombre feliz.*

It wasn't boob-girl that made his groin tighten, though. Not even close. He picked up the beer the bartender slid across to him and took a swallow without taking his eyes off the beautiful woman in a far booth. The beer was icy and delicious, while his body grew hotter by the second. The woman's gaze met his and never wavered. As he walked to her booth, he licked his lips.

"Hola." He propped himself against the outside of the booth, making sure to turn his hips in her direction. Not a bad idea to display the goods.

"Hello." She drew the word out slow, sexy.

Jorge swept his gaze over her. Nice. Her long, dark blond hair fell over her shoulders in golden waves reaching her waist. He did love long hair. Never did understand why Ivy cut hers off. Green eyes peered at him from beneath long lush lashes. Her lips, red and full, beckoned to be kissed. Her skin was so white and smooth it seemed to scream for the pleasing touch of his skilled hands.

He set his beer on her table and held out a hand. "Would you like to dance?" He wanted to press his body very close to hers. Not just gift her with a look at the goods, but let her feel too. Hard to resist what he had to offer.

"Very much." She took his outstretched hand and he pulled her to her feet. Her hand was cool yet soft in his, tiny with long, elegant fingers.

She was even more beautiful standing up. She wasn't very tall, barely over five feet, yet possessed a presence that made her seem anything but small. Jorge liked his women substantial, though he could certainly make an exception for this one. Tiny as she might be, she had beautiful breasts and a small, tight ass. Her hair was soft and shiny as he wound his hands through it and brought it to his face to inhale its sweet scent. Perfection in a petite package.

"I'm Jorge," he told her as he pulled her into his arms, pressing close against her. Her breasts pushed into his chest and his cock immediately responded. He moved even closer, knowing the feel of his big cock would please her. All the women liked what he could deliver, while men envied him. It was just one of his many charms and one he was particularly proud of.

She rubbed suggestively against his hardness. "Jorge," she said slowly. "You like what you see? What you feel?"

"*Sí.*" He moved his hands from her back to her ass. It felt as perfect as it looked in the short black skirt.

"And I like what I feel," she purred as she rubbed her hips against his hard-on. "Shall we leave this place?"

Jorge silently congratulated himself. He was so good, he didn't even have to buy her a drink. He laughed and spun her with one hand. His mama should have called him Lucky. "We shall."

Outside, he hit the keychain remote to unlock the truck doors. The doors clicked and the lights flickered. At the passenger door, he grabbed her around the waist and picked her up. He kissed her hard before depositing her in the leather seat. Pausing at the driver's side door, he grabbed his jeans and pulled. His crotch was getting very tight.

"Any place in particular?" Jorge asked as he drove out of the parking lot. He hoped she'd pick somewhere close. He wasn't sure how long he could stay bound up in his jeans.

She ran a finger down his cheek. "The old cemetery."

Jorge turned his head to stare at her. "What?"

She gave him a dazzling smile and a wink. "I like it a little kinky. Is that a problem for you?" she drawled.

Okay, so maybe he did hear her right. Freaky little bitch. The night just kept getting better. "Oh, no, *mujer atractiva*. Kinky is just my style."

He laughed, ran one hand down her exposed thigh, and turned the truck east with the other. Could this babe get any hotter?

Jorge drove the back roads, turning and stopping a couple of times to get his bearings. The cemetery sat in the middle of nowhere, a square patch of trees and headstones. In an otherwise vast, boring flatland, it was the only disruption.

The sky overhead was pitch black, punctuated by a mantle of twinkling stars and a round full moon. It was easy to get lost when it was so dark and everything looked the same. His throbbing cock urged him to find the cemetery, and quickly. Finally, the stand of trees that defined the perimeter came into view.

He'd barely put the truck in Park when she jumped out to run past several large weeping willows and the veterans' memorial before stopping in the middle of the cemetery. Jorge followed, his blood pumping and his heart racing as he weaved between headstones.

The sooner he could get out of these jeans, the better. "Tight" didn't even begin to describe them. He caught the beauty in his arms and kissed her. She kissed him back, hard and hungry, her tongue thrusting into his mouth. What a tigress.

He sighed as she nuzzled his neck with warm kisses. "You never told me your name," he said in a husky voice as he slid his hands beneath her little skirt. She wore nothing underneath.

Why weren't they getting out of their clothes? The kisses were nice, but it was time to get down and dirty.

Her laugh was soft. "No, I did not."

The last thing Jorge felt was the sting of her fangs as they sank into his neck.

❖

Adriana started at Riah's lips and kissed all the way down her body. At her nipples, she bit, the pain sweet. Riah bucked against the sensation and Adriana laughed.

"Patience, my love, we're just getting started." Her tongue was hot against Riah's cool skin.

Riah was awash in sensation, and so far all Adriana had touched her with was her mouth. She hadn't even used her hands. As soon as the thought flitted through her mind, Adriana surprised her when she brushed a fingertip between her folds and across her clit. A moment later, she slipped a finger inside. Riah was wet and ready. She pulled at her restraints, pushing against the feel of Adriana's finger inside her. Adriana slipped in another finger and moved them both in and out with agonizing slowness.

"Tell me what you want," Adriana murmured. "Tell me."

Riah could barely put two thoughts together, yet Adriana's words got through. "Fuck me," she gasped.

Adriana laughed and slid down on the bed until her face was between Riah's legs. She licked her clit, teasing with her tongue as her fingers continued to move in and out, in and out.

Sensation built inside, growing with each touch of Adriana's tongue and fingers. Riah breathed more rapidly as she tensed at the incredible feelings flowing through her body. She pulled against the restraints and then, when she thought she couldn't stand it a moment more, she screamed and her entire body went limp.

Her breathing was just beginning to slow when Adriana moved next to her on the bed and kissed her gently. She tasted sweet, hot.

"I love you, Riah."

She didn't know what to say, though she knew what Adriana wanted her to say and couldn't. She'd loved once and lost. Wasn't sure it was possible to find love again. Riah always believed her chance had come and gone. Except, tonight something wonderful had happened. This was so much more than sex, although she wasn't sure why. She didn't think she loved Adriana. Not in that way. She certainly loved her as a friend. Yet, this was different from anything Riah had felt in such a long time.

"I…" Riah didn't want to lie or force something that might or might not be real.

Adriana put a finger to her lips. "Shhh. Don't ruin it by saying something very Riah." She pulled the blindfold from Riah's face.

What did she mean? Adriana rolled away and began to untie Riah's hands and feet. She wouldn't meet her eyes.

"Adriana?"

"No, Riah. I mean it. Don't say anything."

Riah rubbed her wrists, slight red marks where she pulled against the restraints. Not a problem, they'd be gone within minutes. It just gave her something to concentrate on besides the troubling questions in her mind. Better yet, she opted to change the subject.

"What about the blood?"

Adriana paused and looked up from the foot of the bed where she'd just untied the last scarf. It hung forgotten in her hand, a quizzical look on her face. "The blood?"

"The blood from the guy Ivy brought up from Moses Lake."

Adriana laughed and slapped her forehead. "Oh, yeah. Kind of forgot about him."

Riah smiled and pushed her damp hair off her forehead. "Well, so did I...for a little bit anyway."

"Okay." Adriana sat cross-legged on the foot of the bed and looked at Riah, obviously trying to concentrate. "I'm confident I've finally isolated the protein that causes the change. Now, I'm on my tenth-generation serum and I'm waiting to see how this guy's blood reacts. I'll know more tomorrow."

Riah sighed. "So nothing yet." She tried not to feel disappointed and failed. Each time she hoped it would work and each time something went wrong.

"No, no, Riah, that's not true. We're closer than we've ever been. At least we know what puts the change into motion."

"But if we can't stop it or reverse it, we've got nothing." She didn't mean to sound bitter.

Adriana scooted back up and took Riah into her arms, kissing the top of her head. "I promise, I'll find it."

Riah wished she could believe Adriana. Unfortunately, she knew how easily heartfelt promises could turn to ashes.

CHAPTER FIVE

Ivy bolted upright when the bedside phone rang and shattered the quiet night. "Hernandez," she mumbled into the receiver as she tried to shake off the fogginess of sleep. She hated these calls, even if they were standard operating procedure for someone in her position.

"Ivy."

Daryl wasn't a quiet guy, and the fact he was speaking so softly sent a chill up her back. She was suddenly wide awake. "What is it?"

"We have a situation."

She swung her legs off the bed, pressing the phone to her ear, with a death-grip on the receiver. "Just tell me what it is. You have another body?" Not a big leap, considering these calls usually came with a dead body. Especially right now since it seemed as if it was open season in Grant County and the prey of choice was human beings. Her stomach did a roll.

"Yeah."

She was already up and moving toward the bathroom. "I'll be right there, just tell me where."

He coughed slightly. "It's not just a body."

What else could it be? More than one? Shit, was the killer getting greedy? She stopped in the middle of the bathroom, all vestiges of sleep long gone. "Okay, so what else is the problem?"

"I don't really want to tell you over the phone."

"Oh, for Christ's sake, Daryl, just spit it out. I'm a big girl." She didn't have time for his pussy-footing around.

Daryl's sigh was long, his pause even longer. "It's another victim like the guy we pulled from the lake yesterday."

Duh. "Get to the point." Was she going to have to drag it out of him word by word? She reached for her pants, keeping the phone pressed to her ear with her shoulder.

"It's your ex."

The three words fell like concrete blocks on her ears. Ivy's leg's buckled, her pants fell to the floor, and she almost dropped the phone. "What did you just say?"

"I'm sorry, Ivy. It's Jorge." This time his words came in a rush.

Impossible. How many hours had passed since he stood at her curb? Two? Three? No way could he be dead. He might be a handsome cheat and liar, but he didn't deserve to die. It had to be a horrible mistake.

"Are you sure?"

"Yeah, I'm sure. I've seen him."

Daryl wasn't the kind of guy who'd play a joke this cruel. In fact, he was as straight an arrow as it came. If he said Jorge was dead and he'd seen him…then Jorge was dead.

"Tell me where," she managed to get out as she sank to the edge of the tub. Her mouth was dry and her body numb. Two minutes later, she clicked off and let the phone slip to the tile floor. So many questions flooded her mind. Who? When? Why?

Most of all why? Everyone liked Jorge. She still liked him despite being pissed at him for not moving on. He was one of those guys hard to hate. Of course, he was terribly good-looking, but he had more than looks. Jorge was a charmer, both his good fortune and his downfall. He liked to work his magic, especially on young, pretty women. Made him a popular guy in a lot of places—home wasn't one of them, hence the divorce decree. In his defense, he had a good heart.

Now he was dead, or so Daryl told her. Her mind couldn't wrap around it. She had to see it with her own two eyes. Twenty minutes from now she would. Ivy pushed up from the tub and turned on the water at the sink. The sooner she freshened up and dressed, the sooner she'd know the truth.

It actually took thirty minutes to reach the cemetery. Though the early responders were talking as she drove up, the minute she stepped out of the car, all conversation fell away until the cemetery was blanketed in silence. Portable lights were set up, bathing the area in an eerie yellow glow almost as disturbing as the unnatural quiet. It seemed all eyes were on her before those gathered around a weeping willow tree stepped away to clear a path. A few touched her arm as she moved closer. No one uttered a word.

Her steps were slow as she approached, and it took all her self-control not to sob. Even in death, Jorge was a beautiful man. Propped up against the tree, it was as if he'd merely stopped to rest. His hands were folded in his lap, his eyes closed. His long, black hair was still in the ponytail. If not for the angry red marks on his neck, she'd almost believe he was sleeping. God, how she wished he was.

Ivy slipped on latex gloves and squatted in front of Jorge. Rocking back on her heels, she studied him. Before she laid her fingers on his cheek, she took a calming breath. His skin was cold, even through the gloves. He'd been here all night. She studied him from side to side. When exactly did it happen? It had to have been shortly after he left her house.

"Damn you, Jorge," she muttered under her breath. Why couldn't he simply go home like any other guy? No, just because she'd turned him away, Jorge had to go out and prove he was still a stud. If Ivy didn't want him, he'd find one or two or three women who did. It was his way. And now, it had gotten him killed.

Even more problematic, this was no ordinary kill. Jorge was dead for the moment, but she was pretty sure this stage would last only as long as the sun hung high overhead. Once it dropped behind the majestic Cascade Mountains, Jorge would become something that made Ivy's stomach lurch. She crossed herself and took a deep shuddering breath. This couldn't be happening. It was so surreal, she squeezed her hands hard enough to draw blood. That reminded her how real it actually was, and a sob threatened to spill from her throat.

Now wasn't the time to give in to emotion. Ivy sucked it up and began to give instructions to the waiting crew. Within the hour, Jorge was in a black bag, sealed and initialed, and on his way to her morgue where her assistant, Carlos Reyna, would tuck him away in the cooler. Carlos knew the drill well and wouldn't leave Jorge unattended. Though he never asked why, Carlos always followed her instructions, and that included making sure the cooler door was always locked.

She'd already put in a call to Riah by the time she made it back to her car. At the open driver's door, she stilled and stared back at the small cemetery. It was such an odd, isolated place to go, even for a vampire. So many other locations in the county would have made more sense to Ivy. So why here? She'd probably never know.

"Ivy Hernandez?" A deep male voice startled her out of her thoughts.

"Yes." She turned and stared.

For a moment, she thought she was seeing things. Too much stress, too little sleep. Except this wasn't a trick her tired mind was playing on her. It was the same man from yesterday. The one who'd knocked the security guard unconscious, barged into the autopsy room in Spokane, then disappeared like a gust of wind. The night wasn't going to end on anything remotely similar to normal.

Hands in his pockets, he held her gaze. "We need to talk."

❖

Riah pressed her luck by waiting so long to go home. Dawn was beginning to crest in the east by the time she pulled her car into the garage. Thanks to tinted windows and an attached garage, she didn't have to be in daylight. It wouldn't kill her, of course; it just wasn't comfortable. It wasn't like she had to prove anything to anybody, alive or undead, so she opted for comfort on those rare occasions when she exposed herself to the light of day.

Truth was, she should have left Adriana's side hours ago. Should have, but didn't. It was hard to describe the feeling of lying in bed next to her firm, rounded body. It had been impossible to simply roll away and leave. Instead, she'd made love to her again and again, each time filled with more passion, more desire. In the blink of an eye, her world had changed.

How it happened was still mixed up in her head. She smiled as she thought about Adriana opening the door stark naked. Well, one thing was certain—she got Riah's undivided attention. She'd had many lovers, but this was the first time one answered a doorbell in the buff.

Through the years, she'd taken her fair share of lovers, but this felt different. By all rights, it shouldn't. Yet, it was. She was terribly afraid to put a name as to why.

Riah left her jacket and bag on the table and walked into her bedroom. This was her special space. Years ago, she'd been at a lecture called *A Room of One's Own*, given by Virginia Woolf, and it had spoken to her even though the lecture was geared toward writers and artists. The need for personal space called to her, so she created it and didn't share it with others, not even lovers. Her home was big enough that she didn't need to. Now, as she did every night, she stopped in front of the portrait hanging over the fireplace.

The woman in the picture was beautiful, the most beautiful woman Riah could ever remember. Perhaps her view was tainted because she'd loved her. The one and only time in her life Riah truly loved someone, except perhaps for her long-dead mother. She'd give anything to have love in her life again…in her heart. It was impossible and probably had been from the start.

People barely tolerated same-sex relationships today. Back in their time, so many long years ago, it was unthinkable. Fate hadn't seen fit to smile upon them either. They were doomed from the first kiss. A single tear coursed down Riah's cheek as she touched the portrait. Then she turned away.

Only then did she notice the blinking light on her phone. Wiping away the tear with the back of her hand, she sank to the edge of the bed and picked up the handset. Awfully early for someone to call today, but then again, death didn't exactly keep regular business hours.

Riah listened to the message and stilled. She immediately pushed the speed-dial button for Ivy.

❖

Working like this was far from ideal. Then again, he didn't see that he had a choice. Things were quickly spinning out of control. Colin had been at this job a long time, and he knew trouble when it came knocking. This was more than a knock; it was more like a sonic boom.

"Who are you?" she asked in a high-pitched voice. Her eyes narrowed to dark slits.

For a moment, his voice caught. She was so beautiful. Even with distrust and sorrow etched across her face, she was a stunner. Curly black hair framed perfect olive skin. Her full lips were pulled down in a frown, though even the frown couldn't mar her beauty. Her jeans, a khaki shirt covered by a light jacket, and black leather boots were sexier than any evening gown he'd ever seen.

"Did you hear me?"

Her sharp question punctured the fog in his head and he shook off the distracting thoughts. It didn't matter how pretty she was or wasn't. This had nothing to do with her personally. Colin had a vampire to catch and this woman might be a critical link in finding her. If she could help him, that's all that mattered.

"My name is Colin Jamison."

"And that would mean what exactly to me?"

"Nothing."

Her hand strayed to her pocket. No gun there, unless it was very, very small. Cell phone, more likely, and he couldn't blame her for being jumpy around him. Particularly when considering they stood at the edge of a cemetery where a dead body that didn't belong in the silent city had just been removed from beneath a tree. Yeah, she had a right to be twitchy.

"Look." He hurried to explain. "What I'm going to tell you will sound crazy."

"Too late, you're already in crazy land in my book."

He nodded. It wouldn't be the first time. "Fair enough. I had that coming. Just give me ten minutes, and if I haven't convinced you, send me down the road."

"More like the loony bin," she muttered, though her hand moved away from the pocket. Her shoulders still looked stiff, and her eyes were narrow and appraising.

Inwardly he sighed. Outwardly, he hurried on before he lost her. "I know who killed this man."

Her head jerked up and she seemed to study him more intently. "You should be telling this to the police, not me. I'm simply the coroner."

"No." The police were the last ones he wanted to talk to. They weren't exactly open to the idea of the undead. At least most of them weren't.

"No?"

"The thing that did this to your husband—"

"Ex, and how do you know Jorge was my husband?"

Colin shrugged. "I heard the officers talking when you were over at the body."

She shook her head and stuffed her hands into her jacket pockets. With a long sigh, she said, "Okay. Go on."

"Again, the thing that killed your ex-husband isn't a person."

"And what exactly do you think it is?"

"A vampire."

He waited for her outburst of disbelief. Through the years he'd been called everything from a wacko to delusional to just plain heartless and mean. People didn't like to be told that something from their darkest nightmares might actually be real.

"Get in the car," she ordered, as if he was one of her staff.

Her reaction would've surprised him if not for the scene yesterday. Last night the three women knew what they had on the table, and now Ivy Hernandez confirmed what he'd already figured out. He wasn't the only one in the cemetery this morning who knew a vampire was the leading murder suspect.

"You know," he said as he slid into the passenger seat.

"Yes." The single word was soft.

She turned the key in the ignition and the engine roared to life. She began to drive toward town where her morgue and office were located, but surprised Colin when she took a left at the main drag. Instead of going back to her office, they headed toward I-90. Once more she surprised him when, rather than pull on the freeway, she hung another right and drove into the parking lot of a large truck stop just north of the freeway.

"Come on," she said. "I need a really big cup of coffee."

Inside the bustling restaurant, she slid into a booth at the rear and he took the seat across from her. He waited until a cheerful waitress deposited two mugs and a carafe of coffee before he spoke.

"How do you know about the vampire?" Colin decided taking the offensive was the quickest way to the truth. Besides, he wasn't in the mood for social niceties.

As she sipped the hot coffee with her eyes closed, he studied her. After a moment, her whole body seemed to relax, though when she opened her eyes and looked at him, her face was still tense. He wanted to touch her cheek, smooth away the care. He didn't. He kept his hand wrapped around his own hot mug.

"I've known about the existence of vampires for a little over a decade."

"No shit?"

"No shit," she echoed, and pushed the hair off her face. "Jorge is my third vampire victim in as many weeks."

That much he knew. The first victim was what set him on a path for this part of the country. Victim number two was killed just hours before he rolled into town. And number three, and a very interesting number three, had him sitting in a truck stop with the beautiful county coroner.

"How did you find out about our evil dark predators?"

"They're not all evil or predators." Fire danced in her eyes again, and though he didn't understand why, he liked the fact that it wiped the despair from her face.

"I would respectfully disagree." He'd followed enough bodies over the years to know what he spoke of. Regardless of what Ivy thought, vampires were an abhorrence of nature. No, not of nature—of something far darker and more evil.

"You don't know what you're talking about." She started to push up and away from the table. Her voice had risen, catching the attention of a few nearby diners.

Colin put his hand on hers. Very quietly he said, "I'll tell you why I think of vampires the way I do, and you can tell me why you disagree. Deal?"

She paused and seemed to mull his proposition over. Then, she nodded and slid back into the booth. "You first."

He finally took a drink of the coffee, not that he was thirsty; he just needed a minute to organize his thoughts. "All right, here it is, down and dirty. I'm a vampire hunter with the requisite tools of the trade. I work for the church and began to train when I was fourteen years old. I've been an active hunter since I was eighteen. As you can tell, I'm a little older now, so suffice it to say, I've been at this a long time. I've destroyed so many of these creatures I lost count a long time ago. Not one, and I do mean not one, has been anything but a blood-sucking monster. There are two left we're aware of. One, right here in your little burg. The other, I'm not sure. We lost her trail some thirty-odd years ago. We don't know if she's still alive but we believe she is. Once I've destroyed the killer in your midst, I'll find the last one and take her down." He paused and took a deep breath. "Your turn."

"You're certain the one who killed Jorge is a woman?"

He nodded. "I'm very sure."

She shook her head and sighed. "Stupid son of a bitch. If just this once he hadn't been thinking with his dick, he might still be alive."

CHAPTER SIX

W hat on earth is going on?" Riah muttered as she stared down at the phone in her hand. Ivy had called with the stunning message that Jorge was dead, and not just dead, but toast, as in their latest blood-letting victim. Now, instead of Ivy picking up the call, the phone went to voice mail. It didn't make sense. Ivy should answer. She always carried her cell phone.

Riah glanced up at the clock and sighed. More than anything, she'd love to jump in her car and drive the hundred-odd miles to Moses Lake. She couldn't. Despite her immortality and tolerance to daylight, she still needed rest. Right now, she was running on fumes, and that wouldn't help anyone.

Inside the darkened interior of her house, she moved comfortably. Outside in the daylight, she'd wear down quickly. Too much sunshine and she'd be a literal wreck. It'd take days to recover if she allowed that to happen. The best choice was to stay here, rest and recharge so she'd be a hundred percent come sundown. Ivy would need her at full strength.

She jumped when the phone in her hand rang. *Had to be Ivy.* She flipped it open without looking at the display.

"Yes," she barked into it.

"Hey, gorgeous."

She was surprised, and pleased, to hear Adriana's voice. "Hey to you too."

"I can't believe you left without waking me." There was a hint of reproach in Adriana's voice.

Riah smiled as she recalled how beautiful Adriana looked as she slept, her hair curling around her face, her body smooth and naked. Her own body flushed with excitement.

"You needed your beauty sleep."

Adriana's laugh was light. "I can sleep any time. I'd have much rather kissed your body all over one more time before you ran off in the night, naughty girl."

"It was morning when I left."

"Dawn."

"Semantics."

Adriana laughed again. "Will I see you tonight?"

Riah grew serious. "I don't know."

"Did I do something wrong?"

"No." Riah hurried to explain. "I got another call from Ivy."

"Oh, no." The dread in Adriana's voice echoed what Riah felt.

"Oh, yes. I'm waiting to hear back, but from the sound of her message, it's bad."

"Well, then, you'll need to see me tonight. I'm just sorry it won't be for more fun and games. I'll meet you at your office as soon as it gets dark." Adriana's tone had gone from teasing to serious.

Riah was sorry too. A taste of Adriana was all it took to make her want more. It also made her wonder why she'd resisted for so long. None of that mattered at the moment. Tonight, it would have to be all business. "Perfect."

"Riah?"

"Yes…" Riah was already mulling over what would happen later when Ivy arrived with the body of her ex-husband.

"I love you."

The three words snapped her attention away from thoughts of the murder and back to the woman on the other end of the line. Except Riah didn't have the chance to respond. Adriana had already hung up.

She replaced the phone in the charger and glanced up again at the portrait over the fireplace. She could almost swear that the eyes staring back at her were disapproving.

❖

Ivy rubbed her face with both hands. It was a good thing she didn't wear much makeup or she'd be an ungodly mess. As it was, she felt like crap and was pretty damn sure she looked it too. Oh, well, some things couldn't be helped, and why it would even occur to her after everything this morning was a complete mystery.

Except she found something about the man who sat across from her unsettling. And not in a bad way. Oh, no, it was more in the does-my-hair-look-good way. Fucking insane.

The air was warm and filled with the smell of hash browns, brewed coffee, and maple syrup. In an odd way, the familiar scents comforted her. Something normal in a world that was far from it.

She was far from normal. Her ex-husband was downtown, locked away in her cooler, and here she sat drinking coffee with a guy she should probably run in the opposite direction of. Instead, she was fascinated. Hard not to be—even if he might be certifiable. The man was a looker. Six feet three, if he was an inch, with sandy hair and the greenest eyes she'd ever seen. And his ass? It made her hands itch. Oh, yeah, he was hot all right…smoking hot.

"Ivy?" He interrupted her thoughts.

"Sorry," she murmured, and blinked hard. *Get it together, chica.*

He squeezed her hand lightly, the same hand he'd now been holding for too long to qualify as a comforting gesture from a complete stranger. She didn't pull away.

"Tell me how you know about the vampire."

It wouldn't do her any good to try to sidestep the issue. He might be volcano hot, but he was also more than a pretty face. A mind like a steel trap, as her mother was so fond of saying. He'd shared with her, now it was her turn to spill. His eyes were steady on her face as he waited. She sensed he'd wait for hours if that's what it would take to get her to talk.

No time like the present. Ivy took a deep breath and plunged in. "I trained under a very skilled and knowledgeable medical examiner. She had an uncanny gift for the field and always a huge list of students waiting for her to pick them as an intern." Ivy looked directly into his beautiful green eyes. "She always taught at night."

His fingers tightened their grip and he nodded slightly. "She was a vampire."

"She *is* a vampire," Ivy said.

He cocked his head and studied her face. "The ME in Spokane?"

"Yes."

His green eyes darkened and his grip on her hand was almost painful. "What's her name?"

"She's not one of your monsters." She tugged at his painful grip, and although his fingers loosened a little, they still clung tight to her hand.

"What's her name?" Colin's voice was very low and the green of his eyes seemed to grow dark as forest moss.

Ivy managed to pull her hand away and began to rub her fingers. She'd have to add "strong" to his list of attributes. "Riah Preston. Doctor Riah Preston."

His brow wrinkled and he cocked his head. "That can't be."

"Of course it can. I'm telling you, I've known her for at least fifteen years, and her name is Riah Preston." So what was his deal? Was he calling her a liar?

He seemed to read her expression. "I'm not saying you're making it up or telling me a lie. It's just that if her name really is Riah Preston, then she's managed to keep off the radar and, more important, it means three vampires are left instead of two."

"You're not going to hurt her." Ivy already regretted telling him. It was a terrible mistake. She was usually a much better judge of character.

As if he sensed her alarm, the expression on his face softened. "I'm sorry," he said. "It's a bit of a shock. You have to understand, my entire life has been focused on stopping these creatures. I've always known what my path in this world was to be and, through much training and education, was armed with the information and tools necessary to do my job. To suddenly discover the playing field has changed is a little difficult to absorb."

"Your playing field hasn't changed an iota. The fact Riah is a vampire doesn't change the fact that she's one of the good guys. Make no mistake, Colin, she's on our side. This isn't a gray area for me, it's very black-and-white."

"You don't really know what these things can do," he stated.

She narrowed her eyes as the flush of temper rose in her cheeks. "You're so full of shit."

He had the good grace to look shocked. "Excuse me?"

She stared at him, hating the way her lips trembled. "I now have three bodies...three fucking bodies, in my morgue, all victims of a vampire, and you have the nerve to sit there and tell me I don't know what they can do?"

"I didn't mean—"

"Oh, stuff it, mister vampire hunter. I'm not the one who doesn't know. You're the one so narrow-minded you can't see the truth." The cell phone in her pocket began to ring and she ignored it. Whoever it was could just call back. She wasn't ready to let go of her rage just yet.

"And that is?" His voice was quiet and calm.

She didn't try for either. She gave her fury full rein. "That you elected yourself judge, jury, and executioner. I don't doubt you have the best of intentions for saving the world from the big, bad vampires, but maybe before you run off half-cocked, you should have all your facts."

"I have all the facts I need."

"Bull."

"Look, I didn't come here to pick a fight with you."

Ivy leaned back against the booth and crossed her arms over her chest. "Then enlighten me, what did you come here for?"

"I came to help."

Of course he did. "You can't help if you don't have an open mind. You need to know *all* the facts before you pull out your holy water and wooden stake."

She thought he'd continue to argue and was surprised when, instead, he began to laugh. At the sound, her shoulders tensed even more. The guy was certifiable. It had to be a full moon, because every head case within a hundred miles was showing up on her doorstep. She obviously has some real bad juju going.

"I like you, Ivy Hernandez," he said when his laughter subsided. His green eyes were soft and seemed sincere.

Despite the desire to embrace her anger like a shield, his words made her shoulders relax just a touch. Maybe she was a sucker for a pretty face. "Yeah, well the jury's still out on you, Colin Jamison."

He took both her hands this time. His touch was gentle, warm as his thumbs stroked her skin. "Tell me what I need to know about your friend, and I promise to keep an open mind."

She raised an eyebrow and tilted her head. "An open mind? You swear?"

"On a stack of Bibles. Now, tell me what I should know."

So she did.

❖

It was like a rewind from the night before. Riah stood in the loading area under the artificial light and waited as Ivy backed up the coroner's van to the double doors. At least it was a repeat until the passenger's door flew open at the same time Ivy jumped out of the driver's side. A pair of long jean-covered legs came out first, followed by the rest of a tall, lean, and handsome man. The same man who'd barged in last night. Now, he stood at the back of the van and returned Riah's stare. With a chance to really study him, Riah finally recognized him for what he was.

Riah jumped back as if a blowtorch had burned her, the reflex sudden and instinctive. She couldn't have stopped if she tried. "Ivy," she sputtered. "What are you thinking? Would you care to explain?"

"Soon," Ivy told her as she popped open the back of the van and began to slide the gurney out. "Let's get Jorge inside first. The clock's ticking, chica."

Riah didn't like it. On the other hand, Ivy did have a point. She shot the man a last hard look, then hurried to the doors to hold them open. "You know the way," she snapped. She didn't direct her comment solely to Ivy.

At the same time, she glanced toward the guard office. Who was on tonight? Hopefully it wasn't Brett. Things wouldn't go easy or simple if he saw who accompanied Ivy in the van. Brett really could be difficult, which was only one reason he wasn't among her favorite guards.

She didn't have to wait long for her question to be answered. A few seconds after the trio passed the guard office, a young man, tall and lean, rounded the corner and nodded to her. Thank goodness. It was Andrew Schneider, the newest of the security crew, and a recent return to the city after a four-year stint in the navy. Things were bound to be easier without Brett. Besides, Andrew seemed like a nice kid. She'd always had a soft spot for sailors.

"Everything okay, Doc?"

She smiled and nodded. "Fine, Andrew, thank you."

Without pausing, Ivy and Colin pushed past with the gurney.

"You let me know if you have any problems like last night. Heard about the assault on Officer Barton." His thumbs hooked in his belt, his eyes moved as he surveyed his surroundings and the two people who hurried down the hall to the autopsy suite.

"You'll be the first one I call." She started to follow Ivy and Colin.

"Doc?"

She stopped. "Yes, Andrew?" Now wasn't the time to chit-chat. Ivy wasn't kidding when she said the clock was ticking.

"You can call me A.J., everybody does." The corners of his mouth turned up ever so slightly.

She looked at him and the smile vanished as quickly as it appeared. He was a very serious young man. "A.J. it is."

He gave her a slight nod and then continued down the corridor in the opposite direction. She rushed to follow Ivy. Inside the autopsy room, she had already transferred Jorge's body, still inside the sealed black bag, from the gurney to the stainless table. Riah stopped just inside with her back to the door. With her foot, she pushed the door open a crack and took one final glance just to make certain A.J. was gone. The hallway was empty.

Satisfied they were alone, she snapped the door shut, turned the knob to engage the lock, and stood with her back to it. They wouldn't have any surprise guests tonight.

"Somebody want to tell me what's going on here?"

Ivy pushed the empty gurney toward the door. "It's a long story and you won't believe it. Or even like it, for that matter."

"Give me a try." Riah folded her arms across her chest and stayed in front of the door. Ivy stopped just short of her, the gurney between them.

"I'm a vampire hunter," the man announced from across the room.

Riah turned her gaze away from Ivy to study the man. Her chest tightened. She'd seen his kind before. Not once. Not twice. In fact, she'd lost count of the number of zealous vampire hunters she'd dispatched over the years. Each time she took one down, the church sent in another. The resolve of those who waited in the wings never seemed to diminish. It was an old and tiresome battle. Heavy on the tiresome.

When she stopped taking human blood several centuries ago, she stopped looking over her shoulder for the never-ending hunters. She'd hoped that part of her life was over. Not for the first time, she was wrong.

Things were dangerous enough without this newest complication. She couldn't deal with a rogue vampire and a hunter at the same time. She looked him square in the eye. "Get out."

Ivy jumped in and held up a hand. "Wait, Riah. Listen to what he has to say before you send him away."

She didn't even look at Ivy. "I don't need anything from his kind. He should be grateful I didn't kill him the second he stepped out of the van."

She might have given up her old way of life, but her memories were a hundred percent intact. Hunters had destroyed too many of her friends through the years. Technically children of the church, these hunters certainly failed to grasp the concept of redemption or forgiveness.

"Jesus Christ," Ivy blurted loudly. "You're as bad as Colin."

The hunter had the nerve to smile. "I said get out." Riah pointed to the door.

Ivy touched Riah on the arm. "Do you honestly believe, after all this time, I'd bring someone here who might harm you?" Her question was whisper-soft.

Riah paused. She wanted to disagree with Ivy, yet she couldn't. What she said was true. Not once in all the years they'd known each other had Ivy done one single thing to jeopardize either Riah's secret or their friendship.

"Do you?" Ivy demanded of her, fingers firm on Riah's arm.

She stared at her for a long moment, then sighed. "No."

Ivy nodded and relaxed her grip. "All right then, give the man ten minutes, and if you don't think he can help, you can do whatever you want with him."

"Hey, wait a minute." Colin took a step back. "I didn't agree to that."

Ivy shrugged. "It was sort of implied when you got in the van."

He shook his head. "I don't think so."

"You don't have a choice. I'd suggest you start explaining." Ivy crossed her arms over her chest and stared at him with an expectant expression on her face. "We don't have all night, you know."

Riah raised an eyebrow and stared at him too. Against her better judgment, she'd humor Ivy and give him ten minutes. "That's a very good suggestion." She looked up pointedly at the clock on the far wall.

Colin looked from Ivy to Riah, then held up his hands. "Okay, okay. My name is Colin Jamison."

"And you're one of the church's vampire hunters." Riah didn't mean to sound bitter but couldn't help it. Five hundred years of hiding from his kind didn't exactly nurture feelings of goodwill. Talk about vampires being killers, these guys came in droves and they killed first, asked questions later. They always struck her as more than a bit hypocritical.

"I'm the last vampire hunter," he said pointedly.

Okay, now that did surprise her. When she was turned, it seemed as though there were as many hunters as vampires. Possibly more.

Of course things change, especially when it involves a time period of five centuries or so, give or take. Still, it seemed impossible to Riah the man could be the last hunter. Then again...

"The church having trouble recruiting these days?"

"No."

She tilted her head and studied him. A handsome man, his eyes told her he'd seen the black side of the universe. Like her, darkness had touched his soul somewhere along the line and left its undeniable mark. Still, she didn't understand why he now stood alone in a crusade as old as the church itself.

"Explain." Riah could hardly wait to hear this story.

He told her then of an army of soldiers that the church recruited to hunt down and destroy all who had been turned to the darkness. He told her of the battles and the victories. Some she knew of. Some she didn't. He held back nothing, including their failures, and by the time his words trailed off, she was astonished.

"You're telling me your church has wiped out all but two of us?"

Riah would call few vampires her friend, yet theirs was a world insulated because of their fundamental difference to mortals. It made them all a strange sort of family. She'd know if they were all gone, wouldn't she? Yet, if he was to be believed, they were indeed. Had she removed herself that completely from the world of vampires?

Colin Jamison nodded slowly. "Actually, three, counting yourself. I wasn't aware of you."

"What are their names? The other two." Riah was almost afraid to find out. Though she despised her dark existence, to think so few were left gave her a feeling of loneliness. It was one thing to choose to be alone; it was another altogether to find herself an endangered species.

"The one I've tracked here, the same one who killed Jorge, is known only as Destiny. She's a beautiful woman with pale hair and green eyes. She's also deadly. The other, we know very little about, other than she was the last child of Henry VII. He announced to the world that the infant, known as Princess Catherine, died at birth. The truth was, his wife died in childbirth and the king, not interested in raising another daughter, willingly gave her up in a game of cards. A favored duke, childless and wanting to please his wife, took the infant and raised her as his own. Catherine was turned after a nighttime raid on her carriage, and we've been hunting her ever since."

The tension in her shoulders returned and a knot formed in her stomach. "Where is she?"

Colin shook his head. "I don't know. Once I've destroyed Destiny, I'll hunt her down and take her head."

"And what about me?"

He looked troubled, and it was a moment before he answered. "Again, I don't know. You're a surprise in more ways than one. If I'm to believe what Ivy's told me, we're on the same team."

"Yet I'm the very thing you hunt. What you're sworn to destroy."

His green eyes narrowed. "Indeed. Let's finish this hunt, take out Destiny, and see how the universe shapes up from there."

Riah raised an eyebrow. "Very philosophical for a hunter."

Colin shrugged. "Hey, it's the twenty-first century, and although your friend here accuses me of being a closed-minded jerk, I prefer to call myself enlightened."

She wasn't sure what to think. At the same time, her heart pushed her toward trust. Truthfully, Riah was tired. Five centuries was a long time. It was about time for something to give, somewhere. Perhaps together with her friends, she'd find what she'd been seeking, or perhaps it was simply time to end her existence on this planet. Colin Jamison might very well take the problem right out of her hands.

She studied Ivy and Colin for a long moment before she made up her mind. It might be stupid but, oh, well. "Let's get to work." She headed to the table where Jorge's body twitched, the black plastic bag moving as though filled with a dozen snakes.

CHAPTER SEVEN

Oh, shit…" Ivy's stomach took a huge lurch and she quickly made the sign of the cross.

Riah didn't even look up, her voice tense. "If you can't handle this, leave now." She yanked the zipper, the sound machine-gun loud in the tiled room.

Oh, yeah, she so needed to leave and couldn't. Once upon a time, she'd loved Jorge and married him on a beautiful June afternoon in front of all their family and friends. So handsome in the black tux with the crisp white shirt, he'd smiled radiantly when he looked up to see her coming down the center aisle of the church in her long white gown and filmy veil. How his dark eyes had sparkled. Whatever else might have happened between them, Jorge had loved her, and for that alone she owed it to him to be here.

She took in a huge breath and let it out slowly. "I can do it," she said firmly, and hoped it was the truth.

"Hey." A muffled voice came from the other side of the locked door.

"Let her in."

Colin, the closest to the door, turned the lock. Immediately it banged open and Adriana flew through like a flash of dark lightning. He locked the door again before coming to stand beside Ivy.

"I'm so sorry I'm late," she said in a rush before skidding to a halt, her gaze flying from Riah and Ivy to Colin. "Did I miss something here?"

"You've missed quite a lot," Riah told her bluntly. "Right now, you need to get the samples and quickly. Explanations will have to wait until later."

"Sure thing, Boss." Adriana whirled around to one of the counters and began to unpack her case.

"I can hold him," Ivy said as she pulled handcuffs from her pockets. The steel felt ice-cold.

Gently, Colin tried to take the handcuffs out of her grasp. "Let me."

She started to protest, her fingers curling around the metal cuffs so tight that her fingers turned white. "I can do it."

"Of course you can," he said softly, still pulling on the handcuffs in her iron grip. "But tonight, I'll do this one."

"Let him, Ivy."

Riah's words were gentle though commanding. Slowly Ivy relaxed her hold and Colin took the cuffs from her. While she kept her eyes on the quivering black body bag, she stumbled backward until the solidity of the cabinets at her back steadied her. At least something in the world was solid tonight.

Everything else was surreal. Kind of like a crappy B movie where fog rolls in and everyone knows what's about to happen but pretends they don't. She'd assisted any number of times securing a body to the table as it began to turn. It was difficult to remember how many times she'd watched as Adriana collected samples and Riah sent a soul to heaven before it could be sentenced to hell. In an odd way, it had become a familiar routine for the three of them. But every other time, it involved a stranger. Tonight this was no stranger on Riah's sterile table, and as things began to unfold, Ivy's skin grew cool and her hands began to shake.

Adriana's needle pierced the wounds on Jorge's neck and the vials filled quickly with deep crimson blood. Done with those, she moved to his arms where, once more, vials were filled. The faint, metallic scent of blood wafted through the air and, for the first time ever, she had to stifle the urge to gag. Stars flickered before her eyes and her body trembled. Oh, no…she wasn't going to faint.

The inhuman roar exploding from Jorge's throat seemed to come from somewhere in the distance. Adriana jumped back and almost dropped the half-full vial in her hand. Only Riah and Colin remained calm. Darkness tinged the edge of Ivy's vision just as a wooden spike appeared in Riah's hand.

She came to on the sofa in Riah's private office. A damp cloth was pressed to her forehead and Colin sat on a chair pulled next to the sofa. His gaze was on her face and he held one of her hands in both of his.

"How do you feel?" he asked her softly.

"Like crap." No lie there, though totally fucked-up would be more accurate.

He smiled and the worry lines disappeared. "Crap is good." He gave her hand a gentle squeeze.

"Easy for you to say. You didn't just watch your undead ex get impaled with a wooden stake." She shivered and felt like an icy hand squeezed her heart.

"You sorta missed that part."

"True, I guess I did, but I've seen it enough times to know exactly what happened. I can still see it in my head as clear as can be." She wasn't sure she'd ever get the image of a stake going through Jorge's heart out of her head even if she didn't actually see it.

Colin's hand was warm as he laid it against her cheek. "If you were feeling better, I could tell you lots of stories that would make what just happened look like a day at the park."

She shivered again. "I know you're trying to make me feel better, but I'm not sure it's working."

He shrugged and offered her a slight smile. "Kinda new at this comforting thing."

Ivy pushed up to a sitting position and was surprised to hear her own soft laugh. "Well, you're not too bad for a rookie."

The fact was, coming to with this handsome man holding her hand was pretty okay. He calmed her and the warmth of his touch was reassuring. Perhaps, in all the insanity, to have someone else get it made her feel a little less crazy.

Riah and Adriana entered just as Ivy swung her legs around and put her feet on the floor. It felt better to be sitting upright and connected to something solid. Colin shifted and turned toward the incoming duo, the chair legs squeaking loudly in protest as they scraped across the floor. She'd have liked to protest too. The moment he moved away from her, calm fled and nervous energy roared back in. It wasn't like the arrival of the others rattled her. No, it was more like she needed him close to keep her grounded.

"Did you tell her?" Ivy asked Riah, who nodded. She wasn't sure how long she'd been out and what she'd missed in the meantime.

"Yeah," Adriana said. "I'm up to speed on the great white vampire hunter here."

Colin's brow wrinkled. "You're not a very complimentary bunch, are you?"

Ivy put a hand on his arm and liked the way it felt there. "We've seen too much strange and dangerous crap to get worked up over one little vampire hunter."

He tilted his head and looked at Ivy. "Little vampire hunter? Little?"

She just smiled and shrugged. "It's all relative, you know."

"Besides," Riah added. "Despite what I feel about people like you, we can use your help. Provided, however, you don't try any of your weapons on me. Attempt to take my head, and it'll seriously piss me off."

"People like me?" Colin's voice grew soft, and it wasn't a comforting sound.

"I thought you guys agreed to a truce?" Adriana looked genuinely scared and Ivy didn't blame her. All of a sudden, tension seemed to crackle in the room like the air right before a lightning storm.

Colin met Ivy's eyes and something flickered. She could almost feel him relax. "We did and I'll certainly honor my word." His gaze shifted to Riah.

Riah studied him for a long moment, then nodded. "As will I," she added as she sank to the chair behind her desk and looked over at Adriana. "So tell us what you've got."

Riah's gaze was riveted on Adriana now, and at first Ivy didn't think anything of it. At first. She took a second look and narrowed her eyes. *Well, I'll be damned.*

Between the time she left here last night and now, something definitely had occurred between the two women. Adriana never hid her feelings, while Riah always seemed oblivious. Sure, they were friends and colleagues in this battle against darkness—just nothing beyond that. Until now. Something in the looks passing between them tonight wasn't the same as yesterday. Oh, yeah, something was up in River City all right, and she'd so be cornering Riah a little later.

Adriana grabbed an empty chair and quickly pulled it close to Riah's desk. "Well, I'd like to say I found the cure," she said in a rush, her small hands moving as she talked.

Riah's face fell just a little. "You said you'd discovered something promising."

Adriana patted Riah. Her hand lingered a little too long on Riah's, or so it seemed to Ivy. Very interesting.

"Hey, don't be discouraged. I've made a lot of important ground by successfully separating the proteins and isolating what I believe is the one responsible for the vampirism. That's some serious shit, girlfriend."

"You *know* what causes this thing?" Disbelief rang in Colin's voice. The look in his eyes said he was far from being a believer.

"Damn straight," Adriana said proudly. She sat up in her chair. "Looks can be deceiving, pal. I'm more than just a pretty face and a hot bod." She gave him a wink.

"Undoubtedly," Colin murmured, and Ivy thought he looked at Adriana a little differently all of a sudden.

"So what's the problem?" This was from Riah.

Adriana turned back to her. "Bottom line is, I can find the cause, but I just can't isolate the cure. I'm now twelve generations in and I really thought I had it this time. At least until I tried it on the blood samples from yesterday's vic. Every blasted one went south right before I came over here."

"So nothing," Riah murmured.

"I'm close," Adriana insisted. "Really close. I've just got to tweak the immunoglobulin a little more and I'm sure I'll get it. One or two more generations is all. I feel it right here." Adriana tapped her chest over her heart.

"Let me see if I understand you," Colin said as he gazed steadily at Adriana. "You think you're a couple of batches away from finding the cure for vampirism? Is that what I'm hearing?"

Adriana nodded, her eyes bright, her expression confident. "No wax in your ears, hunter man."

Colin shook his head and muttered, "Son of a bitch."

Riah stood at the doors and gazed out into the darkness. The security lights in the parking lot cast an orange glow over the asphalt, while shadows from the trees danced as the wind blew through the leaves. The air was fresh and clear with just a hint of freshly baked bread coming from the commercial bakery a block or so away. It was quiet now. Only Riah and one security guard.

Ivy and Colin had packed up Jorge's body as soon as the autopsy was completed, zipping him—or what was left of him—back into the heavy black plastic. Ivy then sealed the bag and initialed it once again. Jorge was ready for the funeral home to prepare him for his final journey. The two were back on the road and heading to Moses Lake well before ten.

Riah's heart went out to Ivy, who, while truly professional all evening, also failed to completely disguise her heartache. Ivy had initiated the divorce from Jorge but, all the requisite hard feelings involved with a divorce aside, she didn't hate him. Riah even liked the jerk. He might have been a player and he might have done Ivy wrong, but his heart was basically good. Yes, he deserved the divorce. But no, he didn't deserve to die this way.

Of course, no one deserved to die this way.

Riah shivered as she thought back on the first years of her immortality. God, what a monster she'd been in those days. If turning into a creature of the darkness hadn't doomed her soul, certainly her actions and dedication to the life did. It didn't matter that she'd spent hundreds of years trying to make amends. She'd cast her lot the first time she took a human life. Saint Peter would not be opening the pearly gates to let her in when her days on this earth finally ended. No, she'd be walking through an entirely different set of gates.

Riah sighed, closed her eyes, and tried to relax. Instead…she remembered.

Rodolphe was beautiful, and even as frightened as Catherine was the first night, her fear soon faded in the face of his gentle ways. Tender, helpful, and loving, he made her feel like the princess she should have been all along. She bought into his charm without fear or reservation because she loved the life he created for her.

The sound of a door at the back of the manor made Catherine sit up. She patted her hair, pleased with the intricate braids interwoven with flawless pearls. They glowed brilliant against her dark hair.

She smoothed the silk over her firm breasts and smiled. The dress was a gift from Rodolphe and she loved it more than any other. The puffed sleeves were gorgeous over the slashed lower sleeves, and the jeweled girdle at her waist was the prettiest thing she'd ever seen. The emerald green suited her and highlighted her dark hair and hazel eyes. She didn't need a looking glass to tell her how radiant she'd become since meeting him.

From the dresser, she picked up a delicate glass bottle. The perfume he brought her from Paris was a light, lovely scent, and she dabbed it at her neck and between her breasts. Smiling, she put the stopper back into the bottle and set it once more on the polished dresser.

As she listened, his steps sounded closer. She licked her lips, a grumble low in her belly. She giggled thinking how unladylike the sound was. Still, she was hungry and Rodolphe always brought her the best meals.

How long had he been gone? It seemed as though it had been days. She laughed lightly. It was more likely to have been mere minutes or an hour at most. It just seemed an eternity whenever they were parted. Being at his side was a joy like none other, and he never left her for more than a little while.

The door to her chambers opened and Rodolphe stepped through, a whoosh of cool air following him. His blond hair was pulled back with a leather tie and a few tendrils, damp from the rain falling outside, escaped to curl around his strong face. She thought of how his hair fell through her fingers like fine silk when loosened from the tie. His lips, full and red, beckoned to her with a slight smile. His knee-high boots were so shiny, the firelight reflected off them, while his fur-lined, calf-length cloak looked stunning over a black jerkin and stockings. She particularly liked the prominent codpiece.

"Ma chérie," he whispered. She loved the sound of his voice, the smooth French of his native tongue. It was sexy, alluring, and sent shivers up her spine. She'd never grow tired of listening to it even if she lived for a thousand years.

"Rodolphe." She rose and patted her skirt. She knew how much he liked her in this dress. How he delighted in slowly taking her hair down and working his fingers through the braids until at last it hung lush and free down her naked back. But, that was for later.

"Wait," he told her before she'd taken more than a step in his direction. Then as she watched, he pulled around a pretty young woman who'd been hidden behind his large body. "Mademoiselle Maynard, may I present Princess Catherine." He smiled broadly, his sharp canines peeking from beneath his lips.

"Oh, Rodolphe." Catherine sighed, tingles running down her arms. "You must stop calling me that." She swept her gaze over the woman.

The young woman was pretty, very pretty, though the manner of her dress spoke to her lowly station in life. It didn't matter to Catherine. It wasn't like their relationship would last longer than a few hours at most. They would not be friends.

Catherine walked over to the woman and touched her perfect skin. She was pale, her brown eyes wide and swimming with unshed tears. She was thin, though not starvation thin. "Please don't be frightened," Catherine said to her, still stroking her cheek. Her face was warm, flushed even. A slight tremor ran beneath her flesh.

"I'm not afraid," the woman declared boldly, though her voice shook.

Liar. They always said they weren't afraid, but they always were. Catherine didn't know why either. She wasn't an ogre. She was probably the most beautiful woman they'd ever seen, so why they'd be afraid of her was a mystery.

"What's your name?" Catherine asked as she continued to stroke her cheek.

Her bravado of a moment before faded quickly. "Emma," she whispered.

"Emma," Catherine said breathily before she kissed Emma on the lips.

The young woman's lips quivered and Catherine smiled. She brushed her hand down Emma's arm while she raised her gaze to Rodolphe's face. His eyes glittered and he licked his lips. Catherine smiled more widely and her heart raced. She loved this part.

The incredible gowns, the parties, even the rich, attentive men of her former life were insignificant compared to the wonders Rodolphe shared with her. He showed her a world she never knew existed, and it was exciting beyond anything she'd ever imagined. Though he brought her comfort and riches, it was the power that sent her pulse racing. Nothing could touch the excitement of pure power.

Catherine tucked Emma's hand in the crook of her arm and led her to the settee by the fire. The logs crackled and popped, the scent of the burning pine mingling with the scent of Catherine's perfume. She sat, pulling Emma down next to her on the soft velvet seat. Rodolphe handed each of them a crystal goblet filled with fragrant brandy. Only the best brandy for a very special guest.

Emma's hands shook as she put the glass to her lips and drank. One sip. Two. Just a touch of brandy—enough to soften the worry lines creasing Emma's pretty face. It worked every time.

When she finished her drink, Rodolphe took the empty glass and set it aside. Catherine handed him her barely touched glass, then lightly touched Emma's neck, brushing aside strands of hair. The skin of her neck was smooth and warm. A vein pulsed beneath Catherine's fingertip.

"What do you want?" Emma asked in a voice whisper-soft, the scent of brandy heavy on her breath.

Rodolphe stood behind them, his hand stroking Emma's hair. His touch was light and loving, though his gaze was fixed on Catherine's face.

She pressed her lips against Emma's ear. "Pleasure, my sweet." She inhaled Emma's earthy scent and sighed. Then she lightly kissed her ear as she ran her hand over Emma's small, firm breast.

Catherine's canines lengthened, the sensation sending ripples through her entire body. The feeling never got old. She tilted her head toward the creamy skin of Emma's neck and, with her gaze still intent on Rodolphe's face, bit down.

Colin watched Ivy out of the corner of his eye. She'd been quiet since they left Spokane, not that he blamed her. How would he feel if a vampire had taken down the person he'd married and left her like a discarded rag doll in a pitch black cemetery? And, if that wasn't bad enough, to then be staked through the heart and beheaded when the sun went down the next day. No doubt about it, he'd be a little freaked out.

Through the years, he'd lost people he knew—friends, acquaintances, and fellow hunters—but never a lover. That'd be tough…tough enough to send him over the edge he was pretty damned close to most of the time already. It'd never happen to him. A person had to fall in love first, and the way he saw it, that was about to happen somewhere between no way and never. Even if he did have the misfortune to fall in love, who in their right mind would fall in love with him? Most wouldn't believe him if he was honest about his life's work. And the ones who might probably weren't the best marriage material.

He glanced at Ivy again and she seemed to be all right, at least as far as he could tell. Then again, it was hard to call. After all, he didn't know this woman. Oh, he'd like to. He'd like to know her really well. That fact dawned on him about six seconds after he met her. The morning he arrived in Moses Lake, as she stood on the beach and directed her staff to pull in the body from the lake, she'd fascinated him. From a distance, she'd been stunning, but up close...well, it was no secret why her husband wanted her. She was beautiful, smart, and strong. Who could resist?

He pressed his eyes with the tips of his fingers and told himself to get a grip. Maybe it was time to give it a rest. He'd been hunting his entire adult life and was very good at his job. Still, he didn't usually find himself distracted by pretty women with luscious curves and full lips that beckoned to be kissed. Nope, he wasn't that kind of guy.

Until now.

She even smelled good, an incredible feat considering where they'd been less than an hour ago and the fact they were now in a van with a dead body in the back. More precisely, a dead body that became an undead body that became yet again a dead body. Still he sat here thinking about how great she smelled and how much he'd like to kiss her. Yes, indeed, he was definitely losing it. Retirement might be on the horizon if he kept this up.

"I don't understand," Ivy said, her quiet words a welcome diversion from his wandering thoughts.

He opened his eyes and looked at her. She stared straight ahead as if trying to drive through a blizzard instead of down a stretch of flat, dry, unbending freeway. Ahead of them unwound miles of road she'd undoubtedly driven hundreds of times before, and he'd bet she could drive with her eyes closed. The only thing that broke the monotony of the landscape was the occasional tumbleweed rolling by on a gust of wind. Well, that and a cow or two here and there.

"What don't you understand?"

"Why Jorge? Why Moses Lake? I don't get why this bastard, excuse me, bitch, is targeting my town. What's so special about Moses Lake to make her detour and kill not one but three people? Most people drive by it so fast they don't even realize they've missed an entire town."

Colin was pretty sure the key wasn't Moses Lake. In spite of the three victims, this central Washington town wasn't Destiny's endgame. Why she was pausing to drop more than a single body here bothered him too, but he was certain it was nothing more than a pause. Destiny was spiraling toward an apex about a hundred miles to the east. Right in the middle of a city that he now knew another vampire called home.

He was as bothered as Ivy was. It didn't make sense that both he and the church would be oblivious to the existence of a third vampire. Centuries' worth of experience kept them informed and on the hunt to finally rid the planet of an ancient scourge. Their records were voluminous, detailed, and very accurate, which is why they were so close to making the impossible happen. At least that's what they'd all believed. How could they be this far out of the loop with the good doc? It made him wonder how much more they either didn't have at all or simply had wrong.

He'd have to deal with the hole in their exhaustive intel later. It was bound to take some time to figure out what they'd missed and where. Even more important was how they missed such a critical piece of information. It made him feel vulnerable. He didn't like feeling vulnerable. Once back in his hotel room, he'd make some calls.

"I don't think it's Moses Lake in particular," he told Ivy, at the same time weighing exactly how much he should tell her.

He could probably trust her. Then again, her very good friend was a vampire so what did that say about her? People simply didn't make friends with vampires. It was dangerous and, quite frankly, stupid. Making a vampire buddy usually ended up making a person dead. It was the nature of the beast, so to speak.

"How can you say that? Three bodies in less than a month? To say that's atypical for this part of the state is a huge understatement. Sure, we have some gangbanger problems, and drive-bys have killed more than a couple, but gangbangers are more straightforward than this sneaky bastard. They don't drink the blood of their enemies, if you catch my drift."

She had her face turned away so all he could see was her profile. It was impossible to get a sense of her thoughts. So, he waited. Finally, Ivy glanced his way, and her dark eyes were stormy. It took a millisecond to make his decision. Despite what he could only characterize as a lapse in judgment for befriending a vampire, he was certain she was trustworthy. He decided to go for it.

"The vampire isn't targeting Moses Lake per se," he told her.

"No?"

"No."

"Okay, cowboy, I still don't get it." Ivy flicked a lever on the steering wheel to put on the blinker and then pulled the van onto the freeway off-ramp. The lights of the town glowed as they drove down the hill and toward the morgue. "If not Moses Lake, then why all the bodies?"

"It's a bit complicated." Actually, to say it was a bit complicated was a little like saying Lake Michigan had a couple gallons of water in it.

Her voice was tight and her back ramrod straight. "I'm pretty sure I'm smart enough to follow."

Colin laid a hand on her arm and the muscles tightened beneath his palm. "Of course you can and I'm sorry if I sounded condescending. I didn't mean to. It's simply easier to show than to tell. Let's get Jorge in the cooler and then I can show you exactly what I have. I promise, once you see what I've discovered, it'll make a lot more sense."

Ivy pulled the van into the loading area at the back of the coroner's office and navigated until she had the rear even with the double doors of the building. Unlike when they pulled up to the morgue in Spokane, she didn't immediately get out. Instead, she studied his face in the orange glow of the loading-dock lights.

She seemed to be satisfied with whatever she searched for because she turned her intense gaze away, put a hand on the door, and popped it open. A rush of fresh air poured into the van, sweeping away the electric tension. "All right. Let's get him inside and then you start talking."

CHAPTER EIGHT

Ivy was aware of Colin every second of the trip home from Spokane. It was outrageous, considering a few feet behind them lay the body of her ex-husband—"ex" being the operative word. Still, it was weird. She was as jumpy as if she was out on a first date.

Oh, yeah, a date with a tall, sexy vampire hunter. Just her luck. Did anything normal ever happen around her anymore?

Sure, he was all business and had been since the first moment she laid eyes on him. Yet, something simmered beneath his very calm surface. Something definitely simmered beneath her surface. Unfortunately, she just wasn't sure what it was and was afraid to delve too deeply to figure it out.

Instead of spending precious time worrying about it, she got out of the van and began to tend to business. At the rear of the van, she opened the doors, pulled the gurney to the edge, and waited for the legs beneath to pop down and connect with the concrete. She tried not to think about the fact it was Jorge in the body bag or that tall, dark, and handsome was right behind her.

"Let me," Colin said as he brushed against her to take hold of the gurney. "You get the door."

The brief contact sent a shiver through her. God, she hoped he didn't notice. "Sure."

Quickly Ivy went to the door, waved her badge across the sensor pad, and waited for the click. When she heard it, she pulled the double doors open and held them while Colin pushed the gurney inside. His arm brushed hers again. She shivered. Again. Damn.

She wasn't any less jumpy when Jorge was safely inside the cooler, the van was returned to its normal parking space, and the office was nice and quiet again. In fact, she was even twitchier now that it was just the two of them. If he brushed up against her again, she'd probably do something really classy like hyperventilate. Some big bad coroner she was.

"How about a drink?" She didn't know if he was a drinker, but she sure could use a nice strong toddy. A little liquid courage or nice sedative? Either way, it worked for her tonight. Besides, it got them out of the morgue. Everything else aside, she was acutely aware that Jorge was on the other side of the cooler door. He might be dead—really dead this time—but she was still uncomfortable.

Colin tilted his head, eyed her for a moment, then nodded. "A drink would be nice."

Oh, yeah, thank the stars. "Come on." She waved in the direction of the door. "I'll drive."

Ten minutes later they sat across from each other in the dim light of Earl's, a local watering-hole landmark, and drank beer from icy mugs. Music played low, some contemporary country singer with a sweet voice who sang about a cheating boyfriend. She thought about Jorge, then took a big swig of the beer and pushed him from her mind.

With smoking banned in Washington, the air in Earl's held only the scent of booze and spicy chicken wings. It smelled nothing like the morgue and there wasn't a dead—or undead—body to be seen. So far, so good.

Ivy took another drink and let the cool, malty beer slide down her throat. It tasted nice but wasn't providing the hoped-for sedative effect. She'd thought once they were away from the morgue, she'd calm right down. Didn't happen. If anything, she was more nervous even when she wasn't thinking about Jorge. It didn't do any good to try to fool herself. She was too aware of Colin to be anywhere close to calm.

She looked around the room, full even though it was a Wednesday night. Earl's was a popular hangout any day of the week, and on Saturdays, it was wall-to-wall. At least there was safety in numbers.

"So," she said after she'd sipped the beer a couple more times and hoped Colin didn't notice how her hand trembled. "Tell me what's happening in my town and why Dracula is dropping bodies in my lake."

He set his half-empty mug on the table. Apparently she wasn't the only one nervous tonight. That made her feel a little better. Little? Hell—it made her feel a whole bunch better.

"I'm confident the vampire is the one who calls herself Destiny."

"Okay, but that doesn't explain much. Who is this Destiny?"

He ran a hand through his hair. "I wish I knew, Ivy. She surfaced sometime around 1600 and popped up in southern Italy around the turn of the seventeenth century. Though she's been on the hunt list ever since, she's beautiful, crafty, and elusive. We've only gotten close to her once before, back in the mid-1800s."

"Don't you and your hunters have hundreds of years of experience?"

"Yes."

"And you haven't even been able to get close to her?"

"No."

"Until now."

He shrugged and turned the beer mug between his hands. "Yes and no."

"Well, that certainly clears things up."

"Hey. Give me a sec."

She wasn't being fair. But that happened after a crappy day. "I'm sorry. Go on."

"All right, here it is in a nutshell. After hundreds of years, we've managed to stamp out all but a few remaining vampires. Now, I'm really close to Destiny and I'll take her down. My order has been busy throughout the years, eliminating what never should have been in the first place. Things like Destiny are not meant to exist. This isn't her time or her place."

His voice was cold, unbending. Ivy knew hatred when she heard it, and Colin clearly hated vampires down to his very soul.

What had made him feel this deeply? What happened to make him view existence in such black-and-white terms? Ivy didn't have the benefit of the knowledge an ancient order could provide, and perhaps she didn't see the big picture as he did. Even so, not all vampires were evil.

"You mean people like Riah." Her voice was low and steady as she gripped the almost-empty mug.

Her words seemed to hit home and he had the grace to look a little surprised. Across the table, he studied her face for a long moment. When he spoke again, his words were slow and measured. "Ivy, you've got to cut me a little slack. I've spent the better part of my life chasing these things down and destroying them. Though they were once human, what they've become isn't right. This," he waved his arms as if to encompass the world, "is for the living."

"Why, Colin? Why are you so certain they're all bad?"

He didn't answer right away. Instead, he closed his eyes and Ivy wondered what was going through his mind. Opening them at last, he met her gaze once more. "Because, I've yet to meet a vampire who possessed a single redeeming quality. At least, in the existence they now possess. Whatever they might have been in life, they're evil in undeath."

"You're wrong."

Colin probably had very good reasons for his strong beliefs. She couldn't begin to imagine the things he'd seen or the evil he'd confronted through the years. It didn't mean he was right.

Since Riah's confession to Ivy a decade earlier, her own world had been colored something completely different. Still, none of it changed the hard facts. Riah Preston was a vampire, and Riah Preston was a good, kind person. Never once had Ivy thought of Riah as a thing, a creature or a monster. Humanity continued to exist inside her.

Colin pulled one of Ivy's hands away from the mug, taking it into his own. It was large, strong, and warm. "Maybe," he said softly.

She gazed back at him and tried to read his face. He needed to understand or they could never work together. "She's not evil."

He stroked the soft skin on the top of her hand. "Forty-eight hours ago, I'd have vehemently argued the point."

"And now?" She didn't pull her hand away.

He met her eyes. "Now, I'm open to the idea maybe things aren't as cut and dried as I've always believed."

It wasn't exactly what she was hoping for. "A bit ambiguous, don't you think?"

He shrugged and smiled. Tiny lines crinkled around his eyes and softened his face. "Old dogs, you know."

Even the slightest hint of a smile made him very sexy. "You're not old, not a dog, and I bet you can learn all sorts of new tricks."

"Well." He let go of her hand and sat back in his seat. "The way things are going, we might very well find out."

"Maybe." In the back of her mind she wished he still held her hand.

His voice lost its teasing quality. "So, back to our vampire."

"Yeah," she muttered. "The vampire."

Colin pulled a folded map from his back pocket, sat next to Ivy, and spread it on the table. He'd used a red pen to make X's across much of the map. They appeared to be randomly spread across the East and Midwest.

As she sat next to him, heat from his body wrapped around her. She caught a hint of what? Cologne? A vampire hunter who wore cologne? A man of many surprises. She liked it—a lot.

"Here are her movements over the last year." He pointed to a spot on the map halfway across the country. "See the pattern?"

Ivy traced the same path his finger had followed a moment before, then stopped. Her hand was a breath away from his, the heat of his skin touching hers.

Though she'd thought initially the marks were random, the pattern became clear once he pointed it out. "It's a spiral," she said under her breath.

"Exactly."

Something tickled the back of Ivy's mind, though she couldn't quite figure out what it was. What was she missing? What was the pattern trying to tell her? Something very important was staring right at her.

"She's heading toward Spokane," Colin said as he tapped the big black dot that indicated it on the map.

Holy shit! All of a sudden the pieces clicked together. She grabbed Colin's hand, her own shaking. "I know what she's after."

❖

Riah destroyed the empty packet once she drained the blood. It tasted bitter and plastic. She hated it just as she hated what she was. That she couldn't survive without blood was the worst part.

She could never completely atone for her three centuries at Rodolphe's side, though she kept trying. For more than two hundred years, she'd survived without a single drop of human blood, and she'd continue to do so until she no longer walked the earth. She'd made a vow the day she stepped on the soil of the New World, and she'd keep that vow whatever the cost.

As much as she hated the thirst, she also hated the memories. The thirst, she could work around. The memories…not so much. Most of the time she managed to keep her mind focused on the here and now instead of the past. She didn't want to go there now either. What happened today had nothing to do with her or Rodolphe. It was ancient history. This was new and something she didn't quite understand. Yet.

With everything put away, Riah didn't need to stay. The antiseptic cleaner she'd used to wipe everything down permeated the air. Nothing waited for her in the cooler that couldn't wait until tomorrow. If anyone needed her, they'd call.

At the security office, Riah waved to Brett, who was back on duty. She wondered how his head felt. He didn't look too bad, only the hint of a bruise on his neck. She smiled as she walked by. If she knew him as well as she thought she did, his pride hurt far more than his head. Guys like Brett, in any century, didn't take well to being blindsided.

Outside, she ducked into her car. She liked a number of things about the twenty-first century, and one was the incredible cars. Her father had been a very wealthy man in his day and she'd had the finest carriages at her disposal. All things considered, she'd had a great deal of freedom in those days. Compared to the Jag she drove now, however, the carriage might as well have been made in the Stone Age.

She was tempted to go by Adriana's house. Just the thought sent a rush all the way to her toes. It wasn't fair, though, not to Adriana. Riah couldn't give her what she wanted or deserved. In the end, she'd deliver heartache. Only a cold-hearted bitch would use someone as great as Adriana and then just leave her.

Still, as Riah waited at a red light, she closed her eyes and thought about the silky feel of Adriana's breasts against her palms. She breathed deeply and recalled the sweet scent of her perfume as she'd kissed Adriana's silky smooth neck. She shivered.

"Enough," she muttered, and opened her eyes. Time to go home—straight home.

Once there, Riah powered up her laptop. She had a desk full of reports she needed to finish. Time to concentrate on business and get caught up.

Instead, her hands lay motionless on the keyboard while she thought about the things Colin shared earlier. Only three of her kind left in the world? Certainly, large numbers of them had never existed, but no matter where she'd traveled, she'd always found another night creature such as herself.

True, she'd been alone in the Northwest for many years and until recently was forced to travel all over to collect the samples Adriana needed for her research. The nearness of the recent kills was frightening for a couple of reasons. She hated death that those who embraced the darkness caused. They fed off innocent victims without regard to the lives they destroyed. If she had the power to change their behavior, she would. It also threatened to expose her. Since coming here, she'd lived in relative safety, and for the first time since she'd been turned, she had a sense of belonging. She hated to see one greedy vampire who couldn't get enough human blood force her to pack up and disappear.

Riah sighed and gazed down at her unmoving fingers. It was silly to sit here and just stare at the computer. She powered it down, pushed away from the desk, and went to her bedroom. From the back of a drawer, she pulled out an old, thin leather-bound book. How many years had it been since she last opened it? Five? Twenty-five? A hundred?

She took it back to her office and began to leaf through the pages. Some entries were simply names. Some had addresses, some addresses and telephone numbers. All the names were familiar and she could recall every face.

Riah took a deep breath and picked up her phone. For a full minute, she simply stared at the handset and listened to the buzz of the dial tone. It was silly to be afraid. These were friends. With trembling fingers, she started with the latest name and telephone number entered into the book.

Two hours later, Riah trembled as she set the book on the desk. It couldn't be. She was tempted to pick up the phone and start over again. Dumb idea. Just wishing something would turn out different didn't make it so. She walked away, her legs shaking.

At the large picture window in the living room, she stared into the night. Stars dotted the dark sky in a canopy of twinkling lights while the moon hung large and bright. Behind her, classical music, Chopin, played low and beautiful. The air carried the faint scent of cinnamon from the candle she lit before she hunkered down at her computer. All around her, things were lovely and peaceful. Her own special sanctuary. Yet inside, she felt cold as ice.

During the last two hours, Riah had made twenty-seven calls. And twenty-seven times she received the same news. Dead. Dead. Dead.

Every vampire in her leather-bound book was dead.

CHAPTER NINE

What was it about this place that made people want to live here? Destiny couldn't imagine one good reason. She stood on the gravel shoulder of I-90 gazing at Sprague Lake, a small body of fresh water in the middle of the flat, brown landscape. In the darkness, it was a blob in the center of nothing. To say it was unattractive was being incredibly nice, as far as she was concerned.

No matter. She wouldn't be here long enough to ask, let alone try and understand. She had places to go and people to kill.

Shifting from foot to foot, she looked around. She was very hungry and didn't think she'd make it without a snack. All she needed was a bit of patience. Her plan was simple, and since she'd done it a million times, she knew it would work.

She fluffed her blond hair, adjusted her breasts so they looked nice and plump in her tight top, and waited. The gods were with her tonight. In the eastbound lane of I-90 red and blue lights flashed in the grill of a black-and-white Washington State Patrol cruiser. Perfect.

The trooper who got out made her tingle all over, even go a little wet. She did like her men tall, strong, and handsome, and this guy was all three. It was gonna be a hat trick for girlfriend tonight.

"Is there a problem, ma'am?" The trooper adjusted his hat as he climbed out of the cruiser, one hand holding a flashlight, the other resting on the butt of the gun at his belt. His blond hair was short and his eyes were almost as green as hers. His voice was deep and rich. A real man.

She batted her eyes and smiled. "My car just stopped and I don't know why." She didn't miss the way his gaze drifted to her exposed cleavage. Never failed. Though she had a great ass, her factory-model boobs were her best feature.

"Did you call for help?"

"I feel so stupid, my cell battery is dead." She held the phone out for him to see.

"I'll phone for a tow."

"Thank you." She put a hand to her breast. "I really appreciate your help."

"No problem, ma'am." He turned and started back in the direction of his car.

Just the move she'd waited for. With fangs bared, Destiny was a flash of lightning. She wrapped an arm around his head and yanked it back, exposing his long expanse of white neck. His hat fell to the pavement and rolled into the dry grass and tumbleweeds of the shoulder. Strong, he put up an impressive struggle. His sad luck…Destiny was stronger.

She sank her fangs into his neck and sighed as warm blood flowed down her throat. When his struggles ceased, she let go. He slid to the ground in a heap of blue uniform and white flesh. He wasn't quite dead yet, his breath still coming in tiny gasps. He sounded a little like a goldfish out of the bowl.

What a shame she didn't have more time. He was a fine specimen, as far as men went. She preferred something a little different, but they could be fun now and again. Riding a thick, hard cock until a big, tough man screamed for release could be quite empowering. Alas, not tonight. Time was growing short and they were alongside the freeway—not exactly the best place for a little fuck and suck. Those games would have to wait for another man, another night.

The others waited as well and she'd promised to be right along. To stop long enough for a meal was okay, but that was all. She didn't want the kids to get restless.

Destiny ran her tongue over her lips to wipe away the last of the blood. Tasty. *Oh, what the hell.* She bent down, picked up the trooper, who hung from her hands like a rag doll, and sank her teeth in one more time. *No sense letting a good man go to waste.*

❖

Colin jumped when Ivy grabbed his hand. It was like a woman had never touched him before. Granted, it didn't happen often, not in his line of work. Most women cringed when, or rather if, they found out what he did. What he was. All that aside, he wasn't even close to virgin territory. His focus on the hunt hadn't been quite that strong.

"I'm sorry," she said as she snatched her hand away.

Great, not only did he make himself look like a jumpy geek, he now managed to make her feel bad as well. "No, you didn't do anything wrong." He took her hand again. She was cold and shaking. "Tell me what she's after."

For a moment he thought she'd pull away again. Her dark eyes studied him and then she relaxed. "She's after Riah."

"It could be coincidence." He didn't believe in coincidences.

Ivy shook her head, dark hair swirling around her face. "No."

"How can you be so certain?" The spiral *was* headed toward Spokane, which was Riah's home, but he wasn't so sure it was all because of Riah. If he didn't know about Riah before this, how could Destiny? She was a lone vampire and he had the power of the church at his disposal.

"Here." She pointed at the map with her free hand. "Each of these locations is where you found a victim, right?"

He nodded. He could recall every one. With each death, his resolve strengthened. The bitch left a long and bloody trail, and his inability to stop her frustrated him immensely.

"I've been friends with Riah long enough to know some of her past."

"And that means what exactly?"

"Riah worked in each of these places before she came to Spokane. I'm telling you, Colin, this vampire is tracking Riah."

Son of a bitch. "You're sure Riah was in each of these cities?"

Ivy nodded. "Crystal."

"So why?" he murmured. Now that she'd pointed it out, it was clear. What bugged him was finding himself this far behind the destructive vampire. He should have seen the pattern himself and, more important, sooner than tonight.

Ivy studied his face, her dark eyes unreadable. "You're the hunter, what do you think?"

Damned if I know. This new piece to the puzzle threw him. He shrugged. "I don't know. From what you tell me, Riah's pretty quiet. She works, keeps a low profile, and doesn't feed off humans. It doesn't seem like she'd be an obvious target, vampire or not."

Ivy was adamant. "But she is."

"I'm inclined to agree."

"So, what can we do?"

That was the rub. Destiny had managed to stay one step ahead of him. Even with this new information, would she slip through his fingers yet again? He'd like to simply kill her and be done with it. Not likely to happen right away.

"Warn Riah and wait." It was the best option he could see.

She pulled away, her eyes full of fire. "That's it! With all your training and experience, that's the best you can come up with? Some kick-ass hunter you are."

What exactly did she want from him? A miracle? He still wasn't quite sure what they were up against. Destiny was an old vampire, and why she'd be so intent on this Riah was anybody's guess. Oh, it bothered him all right. Something was at work in the dynamic with the bitch he needed to understand. He just didn't know what it was and didn't believe Ivy did either. Riah was a different story. He had a pretty damn good hunch that Riah held back.

"Yes." He touched her hair. "It's the best I can do until we know more."

She let out a breath and her shoulders sagged. "Shit."

He laughed. He expected more of a fight. "Shit, indeed."

"Come on." Ivy took his hand. "Grab your map and let's get out of here. This place is too noisy and I can't think. Let's go somewhere quiet and try to puzzle this through. Maybe together we can come up with something brilliant."

He folded the map, stuck it in his pocket, and followed her out. "Where to?"

She didn't even pause. "My place."

"Okay." It was all he could think of to say.

Once they reached Ivy's house, she left him in the entryway while she disappeared into the kitchen, only to reappear a minute later with two bottles of beer. She handed one to Colin.

"I don't know about you, but I'm not quite done drinking yet. Beer's all I have."

"Beer is great." He took a big swig from the ice-cold bottle. It did taste good. Even better than at the bar. Or maybe the surroundings and the company that came with it made the difference.

Ivy took a sip from her bottle, then licked her lips. "I better call Riah."

It was hard to pull his gaze away from her mouth. "Yeah, you better." God, his own mouth felt dry even though he'd just taken a good long pull off the beer. It was like a flashback to junior-high school—sans the beer.

Colin waited on the leather love seat in the front room while Ivy made the call in another room. An office, maybe? The house was nice, a brick two-story with big windows and tall ceilings. The walls were painted a pale shade of yellow with a collection of black-and-white photos on the far wall. He stood and walked over to the pictures. Family and friends, he guessed, relieved to see none of Jorge.

He went back to the love seat and sat down again. Resting an arm on the back, he gazed out the window. It was dark, and no cars traveled the street at this time of night. He couldn't see lights in any other house on the street. It was almost as though they were all alone.

He should go back to Spokane and to his hotel, except he didn't want to. He should be here. No, that wasn't right either. He needed to be here. To put a hundred miles between himself and Ivy seemed wrong. So, he didn't. He leaned back, finished the beer, and waited.

"You reach her?" he asked when Ivy walked in a few minutes later.

She nodded and sat beside him. The love seat wasn't big so she sat very close. She smelled great.

"Yes. I explained what you discovered and told her my theory. She agreed."

"Good," he muttered, not listening as close as he should, though pleased that she'd gotten through to Riah.

It was foolish for him to be concerned about a vamp. His job was to put them down, all of them, yet here he was worried about keeping one alive. What was happening to him lately? It'd be a really good idea not to let Monsignor know about this most recent turn of events. They'd pull him in a heartbeat. He might be the only hunter still on the job, but that didn't mean others couldn't step into his shoes if need be. Yeah, he'd keep this little tidbit of info nice and close to the vest.

"She's one of the good guys," Ivy said softly, almost as if she could read his thoughts. Her hand covered his where it lay on his thigh.

He turned his head so he could see her face. The lighting was soft and her features were delicate, beautiful. Her skin was gorgeous, her lips full, kissable. She smelled like vanilla, sweet and fresh.

"I know," he said quietly, shocked because he actually believed it.

Her dark eyes studied his face, then she surprised him by pressing a kiss to his lips. Her tongue touched his—hot, demanding. He groaned and shifted, the crotch of his pants suddenly very snug.

Riah was still fretting over the disturbing phone calls when she heard a soft knock on her front door.

"What now?" Looking through the peephole, she wrinkled her brow. Adriana stood on the front steps, a long, black coat pulled tight against the cool night air. Not good.

"Hey." Adriana smiled when Riah opened the door.

"Is there a problem?" Something must be wrong with the samples from Jorge. Why else would Adriana be here? But she didn't give off the vibes of someone who was worried or upset. In fact, her beautiful dark eyes seemed to dance.

Adriana stepped past Riah and into the house. "Yes, there's definitely a problem," she said in a happy voice.

Despite Adriana's cheerful demeanor, Riah's heart sank. She'd hoped they were close to the breakthrough they'd been spending so much time and energy on for so long. She closed the door. Might as well get the bad news over with.

"The problem," Adriana said as she slid the coat slowly from her shoulders to reveal her naked body beneath, "was there I sat at home, all alone and really, really horny."

The coat dropped like a puddle around Adriana's feet. Her nipples grew hard as the cool air reached them.

"I...I..." Riah's throat was dry.

Adriana took Riah's hand and placed it on one of her breasts. Her erect nipple pushed against the palm of her hand, hot against her cool skin. The sensation was heart-stopping. She swallowed.

"Shhh." Adriana kissed against her lips. "I'm horny, I'm wet, and I want only one woman. Please don't make me go."

Riah should pick the coat up from the floor, make Adriana put it back on, and send her home. No lasting good could come if they were to take this further. No good at all...

God, she tasted good though. Riah caressed the breast in her hand while she pulled Adriana close with her other arm. She was so hot.

"You should go," she whispered.

"No, I shouldn't." Adriana began to unbutton Riah's blouse, kissing each inch of skin she bared. Pushing the blouse aside, Adriana kissed Riah's nipple through the fabric of her bra.

Riah sucked in a breath. "You're making me insane," she murmured.

Adriana's laughter was light and happy. "Oh, baby, the last thing I want to do is send you over the edge."

"What do you want to do?"

Adriana pulled back and smiled. "Now you're talking. How do you feel about toys?"

Riah raised both eyebrows and studied Adriana, who almost glowed with happiness. She finally hedged. "They can be fun." When was the last time she'd even seen a toy, let alone used one? Of course, sex hadn't exactly been high on her to-do list for quite a while.

From the floor, Adriana picked up the purse she'd had slung over one shoulder when she came in. She pulled out a strap-on, complete with a purple cock, wagged it in the air, and giggled. "Trust me, girlfriend, this'll be fun. Now how about you get out of those clothes?"

A purple cock? Ah, why not—Adriana might be right. Fun could come in all shapes, sizes, and colors. "You're full of surprises," she told Adriana as she shed her clothes right where she stood.

"You ain't seen nothing yet." Adriana ran her hand down Riah's body, pausing to rub her clit. One finger slipped inside and Riah sighed, pushing her hips against Adriana's hand.

"You're something," Riah said, her head tilted back and her eyes closed. Adriana's hand felt incredible. If she lived forever, she'd never tire of her touch.

"And you're wet."

"Can you blame me?" Riah said on a sigh.

"I was more worried."

Riah opened her eyes and looked at Adriana. "Worried?"

All the merriment went out of Adriana's face. Her dark eyes were serious and her lips trembled a little. "I was afraid you wouldn't want me again."

It would probably be better for them both if Riah lied. The problem was—she couldn't. She couldn't lie and she couldn't let her go. "Oh, Jesus, Adriana, I want you so much I could come right now."

Adriana smiled and moved her finger in and out of Riah. Once again, her eyes danced. "Really…"

"You're driving me insane." The words came out in a breathy whisper.

"Well, I told you I don't want to do that. How about I just fuck you instead?"

Riah put a hand behind Adriana's head, drew her close, and kissed her hard. "Oh, yes."

As polite and conservative as Adriana was in the real world, inside the bedroom, she was just shy of being a dominatrix. It was a fantastic change for both of them. After some five hundred years, Riah was always confident and in control. Except with Adriana. It seemed so natural to give herself over to this woman who made her feel fresh and alive.

Enough reality seeped in for Riah to take stock of her position. They couldn't stand in the foyer and make love. Well, they could, but there were better places than the hardwood entry. Riah hesitated only a moment before she took Adriana's hand and led her down the hallway. She refused to think too hard about what she was going to do. Instead she pushed open her bedroom door and waved Adriana inside.

It was time for a change.

Adriana told her to lie across her big, comfortable bed on her stomach with her feet still on the floor. Once again, she tied Riah's hands, then walked around to stand between her legs. She tingled from head to foot and, so far, Adriana hadn't even touched her. There was no blindfold this time, but all she could see with her head turned to the side was the beautiful carved footboard.

Adriana pushed Riah's legs until she was spread as far as she could be before her fingers slid between Riah's ass cheeks. If it was possible, she became even wetter. Adriana's fingers continued to move, sliding in and out of her, touching, and stroking. Riah moaned and quivered, the restraints on her wrists and Adriana standing between her legs hampering her movements.

"Do you like this?" Adriana kissed her ass.

"Yes," Riah whispered.

"Do you want more?" She flicked a finger over her clit.

"God, yes."

Adriana stepped from between her legs and Riah stiffened. "Don't go."

"Not to worry, my love." She kissed Riah's lower back.

A moment later, Adriana stepped back between her legs and slipped several fingers inside her. She moved them slowly as Riah pushed against her, a volcano building heat and intensity.

"Hmmm, I think you're ready." Her fingers pulled away.

The sensation of the cock sliding into her had Riah shuddering and very nearly climaxing. She moaned louder and thrust her ass even harder against Adriana.

"You like the cock? You like the way I fuck you?"

"Yes." She was breathless.

"Tell me what you want."

Riah groaned, unable to say anything. She pushed back as much as she could.

"Tell me!" Adriana slapped her ass.

"I want it all."

Adriana grabbed her hips and pulled, moving the cock faster and faster. Her wrists burned with the rub of the restraints. Heat built inside Riah, her nipples tender against the fabric of the bedspread. She was as wet and hot as she'd ever been, so the cock slipped in and out with ease. She couldn't take it, couldn't stand the pressure a moment longer. Her breath seemed to catch in her throat. All of a sudden, everything exploded and she screamed.

CHAPTER TEN

What am I doing?

Ivy pulled away as her cheeks burned and her heart pounded. "I'm so sorry," she sputtered.

His gaze was intense, his lips turned up in the slightest smile. He looked sexy, which sent a brand-new flush up her face.

"Nothing to be sorry for, although I've got to say, you surprised the daylights out of me."

"I surprised myself too." She didn't normally kiss strange men—even really good-looking strange men.

He slouched back against the sofa and stretched his legs out. As he eyed her, he crossed one foot over the other. He didn't look uncomfortable at all. In fact, he looked just the opposite.

"So what happened?" he asked as casual as if nothing had happened. "My stunning sex appeal? My smoky good looks? What?"

Ivy shifted on the sofa, pulling her legs up beneath her. She ran both hands through her hair and laughed. "No, none of that. It was more…I don't know, I guess it was that you believed me."

He raised both eyebrows. "Do you kiss everyone who agrees with you?"

She laughed softly and looked at her hands. "No."

"Good."

She snapped her gaze back to his face, and he studied her before saying, "Some people might misconstrue your intentions."

"Did you?" She wasn't sure what her intentions were. Only that they weren't exactly what she'd classify as honorable in the strict sense of the word.

"No."

Breathing seemed suddenly difficult and her thoughts raced back to that morning. Had she put on a decent pair of underwear?

Colin put his hand on hers once again. It was warm, comforting. "Something's here," he said, validating what swirled around inside her. "But tonight isn't the time to find out what it is."

"You feel it too?"

His hand squeezed hers. "Oh, yeah."

"Thank God." A weight lifted from Ivy's shoulders.

"I think it'd be a really good idea if I headed back to Spokane."

Ivy jumped up. "That's nuts. It's late and that's over an hour's drive. You might as well stay here and sleep."

He raised an eyebrow, a slow smile turning up the corners of his mouth. "You want me to stay here and…sleep?"

"Yes," she said slowly. "Sleep as in head on a pillow, all alone, with your eyes closed and your clothes on."

"Clothes on. You're sure?"

She swatted him on the arm. "I'm sure. Come on, the guest room's down here."

Ivy was acutely aware of him as he walked behind her down the short hallway. In the tidy spare bedroom, she motioned to the bed. He slid by, not touching her, yet only a breath away. She almost gasped. Maybe this wasn't such a great idea after all.

"The bathroom is across the hall." At least she sounded halfway normal.

"Thank you." His gaze lingered on her face before she turned and nearly ran out.

In her room, Ivy rested her back against the closed door and let out a long breath. What a day. What could tomorrow possibly bring to top this? With a sigh, she pushed away from the door, stripped off her clothes, and crawled into her own bed. She usually slept in the buff and it usually felt great. Perhaps not such a great idea tonight.

After a minute, she got up, put on a nightshirt, then got back into bed. Naked, she wasn't sure she'd be able to go to sleep with Colin right across the hall. She'd lie there imagining *him* likewise lying beneath the smooth sheets sans clothing. More to the point, imagining what his bare skin might feel like pressed against hers.

"Oh, Lord," she muttered. "Not fair."

❖

The phone rang just as Riah and Adriana stepped out of the shower. Riah wrapped a towel around her and sprinted for the bedside table, leaving Adriana to dry off in the bathroom.

"Yes," she said into the receiver as she watched Adriana stroll dry and naked from the bathroom, rubbing her damp hair with a towel. Her beauty nearly took Riah's breath away.

For a moment, she was so focused on Adriana, the words coming from the other side of the phone line were an incoherent jumble. Something finally got through the desire fogging her mind. It was two words: "dead" and "patrolman."

"Repeat that." She was no longer looking at Adriana and her body cooled as the import of the caller's message hit home.

Five minutes later, Riah replaced the phone on the nightstand and sat on the edge of the bed. She closed her eyes and took a couple of long, deep breaths while rubbing her temples with the tips of her fingers. Headaches weren't solely for the living.

"What's happened?"

Adriana came up behind and wrapped her arms around Riah's shoulders. Adriana's full, warm breasts against her back were soothing and she smelled of mango shampoo. What Riah wouldn't give to fall back against the pillows and make sweet love again. That would chase the headache far away. Except nothing was sweet right now, and making love wasn't in the cards.

"A Stater has been murdered." It didn't sound any better coming from her lips. It sent a sick feeling deep into the pit of her stomach.

Adriana's arms tightened around her. "How?"

Riah heard the note in Adriana's rhetorical question. Death was on the wind heading their way. They all felt it.

What was going on? Vampires killing humans was nothing new. She'd seen too many deaths like that to count over the years, yet the recent ones were odd. Particularly in the twenty-first century where experts questioned and studied death at the most minute levels.

Hundreds of years ago, leaving a dead body along the road wasn't as dangerous as it was today. Certainly, people questioned the how and the why, but forensic science hadn't advanced enough to track the nocturnal killers. Today, the true answers weren't much easier, though following the evidence back to the killer was. Most vampires in this century were smart enough to cover their movements and make bodies disappear. Vamps didn't drop one out in the open—unless they wanted to.

"I don't know what's happening," she finally admitted.

"I don't either, but if we don't get a little rest, neither of us will be any good." Adriana slid off the bed and started out the door.

Riah cocked her head and watched in silence as Adriana disappeared, only to reappear a minute later wrapped in her coat, wearing her shoes, and clutching her bag slung over one shoulder.

"You're leaving?" After Riah had made the huge step of allowing Adriana into her bedroom, it seemed impossible she'd just get up and leave.

Adriana nodded. "Yup."

"Why?"

Adriana stepped closer and touched her face with the tips of her fingers. "Because, we both need time and space. You're fantastic, Riah, and the kind of lover I only dreamed of. But I'm not stupid. Expecting you to love me in return is wishful thinking."

"Did I do something? Say something?"

The smile touching Adriana's lips was a little sad. "No, you didn't have to."

Riah's eyes narrowed. "Meaning?"

Adriana waved a hand toward the painting over the fireplace. "This is a special place for you. I'd have to be blind not to see it and I can sure feel it. Why you allowed me in, I don't know, and I'm not sure even you do. But you're not ready for anything more, and I don't intend to push."

"You don't have to go." She wasn't being polite, she really meant it. Everything Adriana said was true and, no, she didn't understand why she'd decided tonight was the night. All that aside, she didn't want Adriana to leave.

Adriana walked back to the door, her hand on the knob. "Yes, Riah, I do. I'll come by the office later."

Riah heard the front door open and close, then the faint sound of Adriana's car as she drove into the night. Adriana wasn't wrong about anything. This room was more than her bedroom; it was a shrine to a love many centuries in the past. She adored it, the color and texture of the room. The smell of the fabrics and the flowers.

In every place she'd lived over the last five centuries, her bedroom remained essentially the same. The furniture, the bedding, the portrait—all were the same. It was comfortable and soothing. Now, as she lay in the silence of the empty room, she wondered if perhaps the time had finally come to move on.

❖

Colin lay in the darkness, his mind spinning. It was hard to gauge the progress of this hunt. It shouldn't be much different from any other hunt, yet it was. If only he could figure it out.

He already knew a couple of reasons why. One was Ivy, and the other a little more complex. This was the first time he'd run up against lay people who knew about vampires, who might be trying to do the same thing he was.

If most people were really honest, they'd admit they were aware of the preternatural creatures that lived among them. But the majority didn't want to accept that level of awareness. Instead, they left it to those like him to clear the path and keep their world orderly. He was okay with that. He didn't need to be called a hero, didn't need the gratitude of the strangers he kept safe. He just went out and did his job.

In the past, he'd done the job alone. The slayers lived and worked in solitude. It was the nature of the mission. Now, things had shifted and he hadn't quite adjusted. Of course, it was hard to adjust to something with an element of the unknown. He just had to keep his mind and eyes open, and his senses alert. The answer was out there and he'd find it one way or the other.

At the muted sounds of his cell phone, Colin jumped. For a moment, he was confused as he tried to remember where he'd left it. In the inky darkness, he fumbled around until he found his discarded jeans. He stuffed his hand in the pocket and pulled out the compact phone.

The number that glowed from the front display was familiar. "Yeah."

"I have news for you."

Colin was instantly awake, a feather-light chill racing up his arms. "Tell me, Monsignor."

It didn't occur to him until this moment that Monsignor had promised to call him yesterday. The monsignor always kept his word. So, why hadn't he called earlier? Couldn't be good.

"Your mystery woman is still a bit of a mystery."

Why bother to call if he had nothing to share, unless… "I feel there's a *but* coming?"

"But, I have a feeling," Monsignor said.

Colin stood, the phone pressed to his ear, and moved to the door. He peered out. The house was dark and quiet. Ivy must be asleep in her room. He hoped. As he walked to the window, he smacked his little toe on a chair he didn't notice in the dark. It hurt like the devil and he sucked in a breath to keep from yelping. Probably broke the damn thing.

After the pain receded a little and he was able to breathe once more, he said, "Tell me."

Colin opened the blinds. It was as smoky dark and quiet outside as in. The tall red-maple trees swayed as a light breeze blew silently through the night, causing shadows to dance on the ground. High in the sky, a filmy white cloud cover partially obscured the moon. No dogs barked, no cats ran. Nothing moved in the shadows.

"Your Dr. Preston seems to have appeared out of nowhere about fifty years ago." The sound of shuffling papers came over the line.

At Monsignor's words, Riah's face flashed in his mind. So pretty, so young, her dark-hazel eyes alive with fire. "She doesn't look like she could be more than about twenty-five, let alone fifty." Which really didn't mean squat when talking about a vampire.

"Hear me out, son. I said she popped up about fifty years ago. From all we can find, she's been a vampire at least that long."

At least? "How much older?" If he were to guess, based on attitude alone, he'd put her way more than fifty. A hundred maybe? Or even a hundred and fifty.

"My educated guess—five hundred years, give or take."

Colin's breath caught. "If that's true…"

"I trust you're following me."

"Yes." At about a hundred miles an hour.

"Too many timing coincidences. Our records have suspicious appearances and disappearances by a woman whose description matches your medical examiner. It could be more than one, but I don't believe so."

All the puzzle pieces clicked into place. "Catherine Tudor?"

Monsignor didn't pause for even a second. "That's what I believe, yes."

It was too good to be true. Both the vampires he sought in one place? Destiny was almost in his crosshairs and he'd take her down soon. But Tudor? Though she was on his mind, as yet, she hadn't even been on the radar. Sure, he'd imagined the moment he'd come face-to-face with her. He'd even imagined how he'd end her reign of terror. He'd just never imagined that he'd like her.

A sound in the hallway made him start. "I'll need to call you back."

He would have slipped the phone back in a pocket, except he wasn't wearing any pants or underwear either since he usually went commando. He didn't have time to dive for the bedcovers when, after a quick knock on the door, Ivy pushed it open. The light from the hallway spilled into the room, placing his naked body square in the middle of a golden slice of light.

CHAPTER ELEVEN

Spokane was large enough, though it seemed subdued compared to other places she'd been. Too quiet for her tastes. Destiny liked places that popped, where people cruised all hours of the day and night. Where drinks flowed and laughter boomed. All the better for hunting.

Here, it was as if the streets rolled up at the first sign of darkness. The expected people were out and about—prostitutes, drug dealers, the lost, the sick. No one she'd be interested in. Where were all the good and tasty folks of this city? A girl did get hungry, after all. How could a city this large be so boring?

She felt the first tug as she crossed the Maple Street Bridge. At the north end, she pulled over and walked back to the center. The roar of the water as it crashed over the falls seemed to echo in the darkness. She bent over the high concrete railing and let the spray touch her skin. It was cold and wet. She stuck out her tongue to catch the drops of water. Nice.

Closing her eyes, Destiny breathed deeply and cleared her mind. She opened her arms and her psyche. *Where are you?*

The tingle started at the base of her spine and flowed up through her body as powerful as a red-hot poker. When she stepped back and to the south, the flame cooled. When she changed direction and moved toward the north, the fire turned scorching. She opened her eyes and smiled. In the darkness, the lights of the tower glowed. The building was old and, even from where she stood, its Gothic design distinctive. It was a castle rising in the night as if to guide her journey.

Destiny walked back to her car, drove two blocks north, and parked in front of the brick building. It turned out to be a complex of sorts, with the castle-like building set as the jewel piece. The courthouse, the police station, the county jail, and other assorted public entities were housed in a cluster much like the fortresses she remembered from her youth. Of course, back then, they didn't have electronic security gates or cameras.

The tingle was now an all-out vibration. Destiny smiled and stepped from her car. Hers was the only car on the street, which unfortunately meant she wouldn't have long. No matter. What she needed to do wouldn't take much more than a few minutes.

In the front of the castle, she stood still once more and closed her eyes. The vibrations coursed through her body. A moment later she opened her eyes and walked around the buildings. At a loading area behind tall, secure gates, she stopped and inhaled deeply. *At last.*

The heavy sound of footsteps announced the security guard. Stealth obviously wasn't his aim. It reminded her of the pounding hooves of her father's mules when the stable hands took them hay. Destiny blended into the shadows and watched.

He was a tall, good-looking young man, who scanned his surroundings as he made his rounds. She expected a man bigger and fatter, but there was nothing hefty about him. In fact, he looked lean and luscious. A tasty little morsel, if only she had more time.

He held a card that he waved in front of a gray pad. A beep sounded and the gate slid open. He stepped through and continued toward the building.

When another man emerged from the back door, he waved. "Hey, Brett, how's it hanging?"

"Same as always, A.J. They don't call me a lady-pleaser for nothing."

Destiny didn't think so. The second man was also tall and young but, unlike this A.J., softer. Of the two more likely to please a lady, this lady in particular, it would definitely not be the one called Brett.

"Anything happening tonight?" A.J. asked as he stepped into the light of the entryway.

Brett popped a cigarette into his mouth and flicked a lighter he pulled from his pocket. "Not here, though I heard they have a Stater down out near Sprague Lake."

"Some asshole shoot him?"

"Naw. Sounds like he was stabbed or something. All I got was he bled out." Brett exhaled a puff of smoke.

"Brutal, man." A.J. rubbed a hand over his close-cropped hair and stepped away from the smoke.

"No shit." Brett sucked hard on the cigarette again, the cherry glowing deep red.

Destiny would like to watch the men a little longer, especially A.J., but darkness was waning. Time to find a place to rest.

She returned to her car and drove downtown, where she pulled into the valet-parking area of the Davenport Hotel. She appreciated the finer things in life—and death—and the Davenport was the best.

The second she walked inside the hotel, Destiny breathed easy. The marble fountain in the center of the lobby flowed with clear, blue water, and fresh flowers filled the air with fragrance. The lobby was deserted except for one tired-looking woman, who pulled a rolling suitcase to the glass doors.

In less than ten minutes, Destiny was high above the city in a gorgeous suite. The bed was tall, soft and perfect. Destiny put the do-not-disturb sign on her door and stripped. Naked, she lay on the bed and closed her eyes. She ran a hand over her breasts, her nipples hardening as she touched them. Her hand slipped lower. As she stroked, she smiled, rolling over in her mind all that would happen before the next night came to a close.

❖

Riah couldn't get settled. Between the call from colleagues in Adams County and Adriana's words, she was antsy. Sitting on her bed with a goblet between her hands, she twirled the crimson blood around and around. It was as beautiful as a fine burgundy or aged port instead of the blood she needed to survive. She longed for the days when it would have been one of the wonderful wines her father imported from Italy.

Those days were long past and she'd found some sort of peace in her altered existence. Life moved smoothly and had for many years now. Her goals were simple…to find a way out and to atone for her past. So far, she'd managed to do a little of both. Her search for a cure was plodding along well, all things considered, and each time she found answers for people who lost loved ones, it helped ease her guilt. It didn't make up for everything she'd taken during her years with Rodolphe, but she'd simply stay at it until it did.

Right now, Riah couldn't allow personal feelings to distract her. Too much was at stake. Still, the way Adriana made her feel was something she'd almost forgotten. Only in her dreams did it tug at her heart and make her remember—until Adriana.

It was a mixed blessing. When Adriana touched her, everything inside came to life again. When she was around her, she felt whole. At the same time, her heart broke for what she'd lost so long ago. It wasn't fair. Not what was taken from her. Not what was taken from her love. What would life have been like if that carriage ride hadn't occurred?

Going down that road again was foolish. Fate had stepped in and changed everything in her life, and perhaps that was the way it was meant to be. From the day of her birth, her life consisted of nothing but lies and betrayal. If her birth mother, the Queen, hadn't died, how different would her life have been? But she did die, and nothing about Riah's life had been right or true since. Becoming a creature of the night seemed fitting in the chaos of her existence.

Except she never truly fit. Not in her human life and not as a vampire. It wasn't that Rodolphe didn't give it his best effort. He was an incredible teacher, not to mention a handsome and skilled lover. Until Rodolphe, she'd never even looked at a man. Her world revolved around Meriel and the love she could never deny regardless of what society demanded. Rodolphe, a persuasive and skilled teacher, guided her into another existence. In a way, she even loved him. Of course, the line between love and hate was very fine.

Riah took a long drink from her goblet and settled back against the piled-up pillows. She closed her eyes and memories flooded her.

Rodolphe brought her roses. The bouquet was huge, the flowers deep red and fragrant, tied with a soft golden cord. Catherine held them to her nose and inhaled deeply. He knew how much she missed her gardens and occasionally brought her the gift of flowers.

Why, then, did she feel so empty? Even her beloved roses failed to lift her spirit. She sat on the brocade couch and held them close, the thorns biting into her skin, making tiny spots of blood dot her chest.

He stood behind her and caressed her shoulders. "Ma chérie," he whispered in her ear as he dropped kisses along her neck. "You like the roses?"

"Yes, Rodolphe, they're very beautiful."

"Like you." He used a finger to turn her face to his and kissed her softly.

His hands loosened the laces of her dress and slid the gown off her shoulders after he took the roses and set them aside. He licked the blood from her skin, then lowered his mouth to a bared breast. Catherine closed her eyes and allowed sensations to wash over her. He nipped lightly and she shuddered.

"Come," he said when he raised his head.

She took his offered hand, stood, and stepped out of her gown. He went down the hallway and she followed him to their bedchamber. Next door, she heard the soft cry of the child, the other gift he'd brought her this night.

The child was beautiful, no more than a year old, with pale blue eyes and flawless skin. Earlier, Rodolphe proudly presented Catherine the infant, a delicacy rarely taken by any vampire. Children were forbidden, a vampire law unspoken yet universally understood. Rodolphe heeded neither man's law nor vampire law.

He was standing in the middle of the room, naked and aroused. Catherine didn't think she'd ever seen a more handsome man and never would've believed she'd want a man like she did Rodolphe. It was more than the fact he was her maker; he was charismatic and alluring, a lover like no other. Though not a day went by she didn't long for Meriel, she found some satisfaction in the touch of her lover.

Inside the door, she paused and reached behind to take hold of the weapon propped against the wall. Firelight reflected off the gleaming blade. Caught up in the passion of the moment, Rodolphe didn't notice. It was so heavy in her hands.

She closed the space between them. Tears blurred her vision as she brought her arms up, holding the sword with both hands. A confused look, one she'd never seen before, crossed his face. As realization dawned, darkness veiled his expression. One hand came up, the silver ring with the flashing ruby, reaching out.

She didn't hesitate. With all her power as both a vampire and a woman, she stepped into the swing. When his severed head hit the ground, it rolled across the stone floor, coming to rest on the lush bearskin rug laid out in front of the fireplace. Catherine turned away. The sword slipped from her fingers. In the next room, the child cried.

Riah rubbed her face. The goblet tipped over on the duvet and a large red stain spread. She hated remembering and most of the time was good at blocking the memory. Some nights her best intentions weren't good enough and it all came back. Like tonight.

Even hundreds of years later, Riah wondered, as she often did, about the child. Did she ever know how close she came to death? Riah had left the infant on the steps of the local church in the hope she'd be well cared for. Then she disappeared. Catherine ceased to exist that night.

However, Riah was never really free of Catherine. Recollections haunted her. Emotions assailed her. Guilt imprisoned her. No matter how far she ran or how many amends she tried to make, an emptiness inside refused to be filled.

Until now, which scared her more than anything.

❖

"Perdón!" Ivy wanted to be anywhere but here at the moment. No graceful method of exit came to her, so she stood in the open doorway and fidgeted. Uncomfortable didn't even begin to describe it.

"You're sorry about what?" Colin asked calmly, as if she hadn't just walked into his room where he stood stark naked. Yeah, that happened every day.

"I shouldn't have barged in."

He didn't move, the light from the hallway acting like a spotlight designed just for him. "Freudian slip, maybe?"

"You're not going to make this easy, are you?"

His smile was slow, sexy, and a single eyebrow rose. "Not a chance."

God, he looked good. In clothes, he was hot. Out of them…he was some kind of eye-candy. His legs were about a mile long and his flat stomach was topped by a broad chest. The term *six-pack* jumped to mind. Light-colored hair sprinkled his chest and trickled down to where it made a nice thick patch around his cock. She told herself to keep her eyes up and failed.

"See anything you like?" he drawled.

His words did what her self-control couldn't—snap her gaze up to his face. If the heat she felt was any indication, the flush that raced up her neck and face had to glow like burning embers. Great. Just fucking great.

"I…I heard a phone ring." *Lame, Ivy. Real lame.*

He held out his hand, a cell phone between his thumb and forefinger. "The boss called."

"Anything important?" She wondered what kind of boss he meant.

He took a step toward her. "Nothing we have to worry about right now." His voice was low and soft.

"Well, then, I'll let you get back to bed." She took a step back.

"Alone?"

Ivy took another step back. "It's probably a good idea."

"Were you sleeping?" He tossed the cell phone and stepped closer.

"No."

"Me either." He closed the gap between them.

Her back was to the wall. "I should go."

"You should stay."

Heat rolled off his skin. She should turn around and run to her room, except it was the last thing she wanted to do. She wanted to throw her nightshirt off and jump his bones. She wanted to feel that heat pressed against her bare skin.

"I don't sleep around." God, even her voice shook.

His eyes were steady. "Neither do I."

"Then what's this?" She waved her hands.

"I don't know and I don't care. All I know is I want you and I'm pretty damn sure you want me. Tell me I'm wrong, and I'll go back to bed alone." He placed his hands on the wall over her head and leaned close.

She couldn't stand it any longer. Ivy touched his face, the fine stubble on his cheek rough against her fingertips. "You're not wrong."

His mouth was on hers, lips, tongue, even the light brush of teeth. It brought a whimper from her throat.

She let her hands come up to touch him, following the flow of his body from his shoulders to the smooth lines of his ass. He pressed against her, the hardness of his cock hot through the thin fabric of her nightshirt.

He felt good, smelled wonderful, and kissed her like she'd never been kissed before. It would probably be wise to go back to her room, only she wasn't about to turn tail and hide. Something that felt this good wasn't the kind of thing to run away from.

Instead, she melted into him. The message was as clear as if she'd screamed *take me, baby, take me.* Desire flushed her skin in a blanket of warmth. She needed him as much as she wanted him.

He reached down to the hem of her shirt and broke the kiss long enough to pull it over her head. It fluttered to the floor somewhere in the room. His skin was hot against hers and once again she whimpered. Hand in hand, he drew her to the bed, and as she lay back against the pillows, he paused to gaze down at her.

"You're so beautiful." He brushed the hair from her face.

Ivy traced a finger down his hip. "You aren't so hard to look at yourself."

"Ah, the magic of poor light."

"I don't believe it."

"It hides the scars."

"Wouldn't matter," she told him as she drew him down on top of her.

He kissed her, his tongue parting her lips. The kiss was deep, passionate, intoxicating. She ran her hands down his body, settling on the cheeks of his ass. Round and firm, they felt divine against her palms. His cock pressed against her and she raised her hips to meet him.

"Are you sure?" he murmured.

"Completely."

He came into her slowly, joining them inch by inch. She was wet, hot, and ready. Gentle at first, he seemed to hesitate. Ivy didn't want gentle. She wanted him hard, fast, and now.

Seeming to sense her thoughts, Colin groaned and moved against her with a fierceness that mirrored her own need. Just this side of rough, he moved with her until something broke inside and she screamed, arching her back and digging her nails into his back. A moment later, he gave one final thrust and shuddered.

Collapsing against her, Colin gasped, his chest heaving. "Oh, my God. I think you might've just killed me."

"That bad?" she said against his cheek.

"No. That good, even if it was a quickie."

She smoothed the damp hair from his face. "Not exactly what I'd call a quickie."

He rolled next to her and propped his head on a hand. "What would you call it then?"

"An explosion."

He laughed, the sound breathless. "That it was."

CHAPTER TWELVE

H ow did you become a vampire hunter?"
Colin was on his back, relaxed after their second go-around. This time, it had been slow, easy, and wonderful. She tasted good. She felt even better. He could lie here forever and it'd be just fine.

In the heat of their passion, the hallway light remained on and still spilled into the bedroom. He could see her body as she stretched out next to him, serene and beautiful. Though he'd never been in love before, he suspected it felt something like this.

"Hmm," he muttered, close to sleep for the first time since he'd crawled into Ivy's guestroom bed.

She ran a finger down his cheek, to touch his lips. "How did you become a vampire hunter? I mean, really, Colin, you didn't just wake up one morning and decide to track down and destroy creatures of the night."

"True." He turned and kissed her cheek.

"Most people don't even believe vampires exist."

"True again."

He was stalling. Sleep was suddenly far away. He kept his eyes closed and pretended to be still dozing. He was afraid to give up the act. Beyond the monsignor and several hunters he'd apprenticed under, he'd never shared his story. The thought of doing it now made his stomach roll. If he just lay quiet and pretended to be sleepy, maybe she'd let it go.

Ivy stroked his chest, her small hand warm and soothing. He liked the way it felt against his skin. "You don't have to tell me if you'd rather not."

Oh, what the heck. His pretense at sleep probably didn't fool her anyway. "I was twelve years old when a vampire killed my parents and my sister." His mouth was dry as the words pushed past his lips. It was even harder than he thought to say the words out loud.

She gasped and put a hand to her heart. "Oh, good lord, Colin. I'm so sorry."

In his head he could still see the flashing lights and somber faces he'd encountered outside his house. The entire street had been lit up like Christmas, except there had been nothing even close to holiday cheer in the gathering.

"It wasn't much more than the luck of the draw I didn't die that night as well. If I hadn't spent the night with my buddy, I'd be dead too. When I came home, police cars and social workers were everywhere. I wanted to go in the house to my family, but they held me back."

"Terrible." She pressed a kiss to his cheek.

He ran both hands through his hair, his mind full of memories he'd rather not have. "It didn't feel real, which is why I begged to see my family. I wanted to see, to understand. I never got to. At first, nothing made any sense. Not until the monsignor stepped in. He was the only one who found a way to help me. He didn't try to protect me from the truth. He just gave it to me in a way I could understand it."

He remembered the first time he saw Monsignor Dobrescu. To a twelve-year-old, he appeared ancient with his silver hair and fine lines around his smoky gray eyes. Thinking back now, Colin realized he couldn't have been more than fifty. Hard to believe twenty-five years had elapsed since then. In some ways, it felt as though it happened yesterday and, in other ways, a thousand years ago.

Impressions change over time, and while Monsignor seemed prehistoric to his adolescent self, he was a man who barely showed his age now. Colin only hoped he would look so good when he hit his mid-seventies. Except he didn't think he'd be that lucky. Some days he felt about eighty now. What would he feel like when he actually did get there? If he did.

He brought his thoughts back around to the story and continued, stroking the smooth skin of Ivy's back. "The monsignor was special and he took control of my life. He gave me a sense of direction nobody else was able to. He understood what I needed and when I needed it."

"No one stepped up to take you in?" Her hand rested on his chest and her fingers stroked the fine hair that trailed down his flat belly. It sent shivers through him. "What about the rest of your family?"

"I didn't have anyone. Both of my parents were only children, and their parents were either gone or too old to care for me. As it turned out it was probably a good thing I went with Monsignor, because my only living grandfather died just eighteen months after the rest of my family. I'd have had just enough time to get really attached to him before he died too. And, after all that, I'd have still ended up in the same boat."

"That's so sad." She hugged him and kissed his shoulder.

"Yes and no."

"Yes and no?"

"Don't get me wrong. I'll miss my parents and my sister until the day I die. I'll always wonder what my life might have been like if they'd lived. At the same time, Monsignor gave me purpose—a really important purpose. All of my adult life, I've felt as though this is where I was destined to be. I'm an invisible soldier in a war most people don't even know is being waged. I have the skills and, after the loss of my family, I have the motivation."

She began to stroke his chest again. "You're a warrior."

"Yes, I fight and I win. I've been winning for a very long time now and, finally, I'm so close I can feel the end coming. It's empowering in a very strange way. It's as if I'm making up for spending the night with my buddy and not dying with my family."

Ivy shivered against him. "I don't even want to think about that."

"I'm not done though. I'll finish what they started."

She put her cheek to his chest. "But if you finally destroy the last vampire, what'll you do with your life then?"

The same question had run through his mind at least a thousand times. Each time the thought arose, he pushed it aside. It didn't matter what became of him. Making the world a better place so others, like himself, didn't have to face the world alone, did. Despite his deep connection with Monsignor and the church, the reality of his life was a bitter loneliness. He worked, lived, and would, in all likelihood, die alone. He didn't wish his life on anyone.

Except, all of a sudden, he didn't feel as though he was in the world by himself. It was as if his life had been leading him here all along. Yes, he was on the trail of a vampire, but it seemed at this moment as though the hunt wasn't the ultimate endgame.

"I don't know," he said after a long pause. "I guess I'll have to take the AA approach and live my life one day at a time." He really didn't know how to do anything else. He hadn't gone to college. He'd never held a real job. It'd be a brand-new world.

Ivy shivered. "That'd be scary."

"Yeah, it'll be scary to me too, but I don't know what else to do. I've done this for so long, I've never given myself a chance to even think about what else I might do with my life. First things first, though. There are still a few vampires out there, which means I still have a job."

Ivy sighed and hugged him closer. "Then we'd better try for a little sleep or we'll be toast later on. We won't be good to anyone if we're asleep on our feet."

He kissed the top of her head. He loved the way she smelled and how warm she felt snuggled tight to him. "Good idea. Go to sleep, little angel."

She laughed softly. "Not many people I know would call me a little angel. I can think of a few other names, but *angel* isn't one of them."

"They don't know you then."

"Ah, you're just feeling generous because you got lucky."

"I don't think it was luck, Ivy," he whispered into her hair.

She sighed, pushed up on one elbow, and studied his face. "No," she murmured, and smiled slowly. "Maybe not luck." She kissed him on the lips, then stretched out next to him again, snuggling tight against him.

It wasn't long before he could feel her peaceful, even breathing. Despite her protests to the contrary, she slept like an angel, with her head still on his chest and an arm slung over his stomach. He tightened his arms around her as he stared at the ceiling.

Sleep eluded him. Not a big mystery considering the turbulent thoughts racing through his mind. While he and Ivy made love, it was easy to push his troubling conversation with Monsignor to the back of his mind. Now, every word Monsignor said roared back into his consciousness like a load of bricks dropping on his head.

Before Ivy, his world was black and white. Vampires were bad and hunters were good. Black and white.

Now, he wondered how he'd be able to tell Ivy her friend wasn't who she believed her to be. Not even close. Doctor Riah Preston wore a carefully constructed mask, and behind it was a vampire he'd hunted for the last quarter century. That wasn't the worst of his problems either. If he couldn't figure out how to tell Ivy her friend Riah was an imposter, how would he be able to explain to Ivy why he had to kill her?

Riah was in the office early for her. The sun was just beginning to set when she pulled out of her driveway and headed for the Public Safety Building. She'd rested, nourished herself, and taken a long, hot shower. If nothing else, she smelled good and looked put-together. No one would have a clue how rattled she was.

For the third time in as many days, she called and left Ivy a voice mail asking her to come to the office in Spokane. Even though it was over two hundred miles round trip, it was one of those things that couldn't be helped. Given what was happening lately, she needed the few and the trusted around her. Ivy was the best person

Riah had ever known to bounce thoughts and theories off. She had a great, quick, open mind.

In contrast, she trusted Colin Jamison only by default, but she didn't like having to. She preferred to call the shots on who she did or didn't share her secret with. Telling the wrong person could be fatal.

Through the years, she'd had friends, vampire friends, who made tragic choices in confidants, literally costing them their heads. Though Riah didn't want to live forever, she didn't want a stake through the heart or a sword to separate her head from her shoulders.

Strange as it sounded, she wanted to age like a regular mortal, to grow old and fade away as she should have done so many centuries ago. Never again did she want to stay young and beautiful while a dear friend or someone she loved withered and died. If Adriana was successful, she might very well get her wish.

If not…

Not now. She refused to think about the possibility of that scenario. She needed to focus on the deaths piling up on her doorstep. Someone was littering the I-90 corridor with bodies and she wanted to know who and why. This last murder was even worse than Jorge, if that was possible. To take a Washington State Patrolman, and out in the open alongside the freeway, took some serious guts. Or was seriously stupid.

Riah didn't believe this killer was stupid. The murder of the patrolman had a cold, calculated feel. The vampire responsible for these killings, this Destiny, if Colin was right, seemed to take pleasure in delivering death. She knew the type well. Destiny wasn't the first vampire to possess what this century called a god complex.

Rodolphe had the same kind of arrogance. He believed himself untouchable. If he'd lived long enough, he would've been a huge fan of Friedrich Nietzsche. He'd have framed the "superior men have no moral boundaries" quote or had it carved in marble. Rodolphe not only believed he was a superior man, but a superior vampire. He killed without regard to any living being or threat to his own existence. The world, in his eyes, revolved around him. These days, they'd label him a narcissist.

Until the child, his attitude worked for him. Despite his unwavering belief in his own superiority, even Rodolphe could go too far. Though he possessed no boundaries, others did. The one thing he didn't count on was Riah and her own lingering morality.

The vampire so wanton in her killing now was bound to have a weak point. Could she be lured in close enough to find it? It was a long shot. Then again, her path did seem to be taking her right into the heart of Riah's city. If that was the case, maybe she, like Rodolphe, would make a fatal misstep. Riah would be ready for her.

"Hey, Doc," A.J. said as he stuck his head in the door of her office. "Everything all right?"

She nodded. "Just fine, A.J. Thanks for checking." Hopefully, he wouldn't stick around.

"Just doing my job, Doc." He rested his hand on the holster at his waist as his fingers stroked the butt of his gun.

"Thank you anyway." She picked up a file. Would he get the hint? She had the distinct feeling he sensed the unease in the air, so heavy it was almost tangible.

The gods were with her. A.J. nodded and turned away. A nice, dedicated young man, and one very much in the way tonight.

A moment later, another soft tap on the door. Jesus, what did he want now? She was about to snap when Adriana breezed in, smiling big. Riah bit back the cranky comment she was about to spit out.

"I hope you have good news because I could use it," Riah said. She put the unopened file back down on her desk. She'd never intended to work on it anyway.

Adriana walked up to Riah, threw her arms around her, and hugged her tight. "I think I've got it."

"It?"

"Yeah." Adriana grinned, taking both of Riah's hands in hers. "It—as in the cure."

Riah quickly shifted away from thinking about the rogue vampire to considering the possibilities she'd imagined for so long. She didn't want to let her hopes soar, too afraid of the fall if Adriana's prediction turned out to be premature or outright wrong. Still, if the possibility existed after all these centuries to walk as a human again...

"You're certain?" She was surprised at how her voice cracked. Adriana nodded. "Remember the other night when I told you I thought I was only a generation or two away from the answer?"

Riah nodded.

"I got enough of Jorge's blood to do three trials and all three were successful."

It seemed too good to be true. Hearing the words now made Riah's heart race and all the craziness of the last few weeks unimportant. She tingled from head to foot.

"I can't believe it," she whispered.

"Oh, you can believe it, sister. Adriana the great has done it! All I need now is another sample."

The tingle shifted from excitement to dread. "Why? If you've found it, why not use it on me?"

Adriana shook her head. "No way. Not yet. Not until I'm sure. I don't want Jorge's blood to have some anomaly that made the magic happen. I have to be one hundred and ten percent sure it's the real deal. If I can get another sample I can run it again. If the results remain constant, it's gold."

Riah didn't wish death at a vampire's hand on anyone, yet for the first time in several hundred years, she was almost glad a vampire had made a kill. The state trooper lying in her cooler would give Adriana the samples she needed to duplicate her experiment. Riah could hardly process what Adriana might soon be able to do for her. She'd be human again for the first time in half a millennia.

"Ned Stratton, the Adams County Prosecuting Attorney/ Coroner, called in the murder of a WSP Trooper last night. He's in my cooler," Riah told Adriana.

"The vamp got him?"

"Yes."

"Crap, sucks for the trooper."

Her lover did have a way with words. "Yes, it does."

Adriana's eyes were bright. "It sucks that one of our state's finest was taken down just because he was doing his job, but his death will make a difference."

Leave it to Adriana to put a positive spin on a tragedy. "I suppose so."

Adriana started toward the door. "Let me get my bag out of my car, then let's bleed him and I'll get to work."

❖

Ivy awoke alone. In a way, she was glad. The night had been glorious and Colin was a great lover. No, scratch that. Fantastic lover. Just thinking about him made her tingle all over. Where did a vampire hunter learn to use his tongue like that?

Being with him was also surreal. She barely knew him, yet she'd jumped in bed with him like she'd never been with another man. She should feel embarrassed, but she didn't. Quite the contrary. She could hardly wait to see him again.

Ivy hugged his pillow to her face and inhaled his scent. A sigh escaped her lips, then suddenly she laughed. What a girl she was. In real life, she was a very serious and ultra-professional coroner. Behind the blinds of her own home, she turned into a complete cream puff that melted when a sexy man ran his tongue down her body. Today, cream puff worked for her. She smiled, kissed the pillow, and tossed it aside. As appealing as it might be, she couldn't spend the entire day in bed.

After a shower, Ivy went to the kitchen where Colin had left a note on the counter. She smiled as she read his tidy script. He'd gone back to Spokane to try to figure out where Destiny was headed. He also left his cell-phone number. No endearments. No apologies— thank God. She liked him better by the minute.

Her cell phone lay on the counter, with the image of an envelope on the display. Maybe Colin had changed his mind and decided he needed to talk to her after all? She quickly punched in her code and listened to the message. It wasn't Colin.

Riah's voice sounded strained and her message was troubling for more than one reason. The bodies continued to pile up, except now they seemed to be moving east. If Ivy were to guess, this Destiny was likely in Spokane already. According to Riah's message, a dead

Washington State Trooper was found on the outskirts of Sprague, about forty miles west of Spokane. The elusive vampire was on the move, so Moses Lake was probably safe for a while.

Today was Saturday and no one expected Ivy in the office, despite her habit of showing up anyway. Murders always guaranteed her appearance, although fortunately in Moses Lake those were few. Accidents were more common. Sometimes she came in on the weekends for those, and sometimes she let one of the deputy coroners handle them.

Today was as good as any to delegate. It was one of the reasons she'd been able to sleep so late. After a couple of days with little to no sleep and a late night playing footsy with Colin, she'd been exhausted. Now, she was wide-awake, fully refreshed, and needing a good cup of coffee even if it was late afternoon.

Ten minutes later she pulled into the Starbucks just off I-90 and ordered their biggest latte. Now she could face the rest of the day. She was headed for Spokane a few minutes later.

Her cell phone rang just about the time she passed the starch plant, and she groaned at the sound of Phil's voice. Between him and the stench of the plant, Ivy almost retched. With effort, she pushed down the urge and tried to sound civil.

She bypassed a greeting. "You know I can't say anything."

"Ivy, buddy, old pal, you know I gotta ask." His voice was too sweet to take seriously.

"Look, Phil, I understand you're only doing your job—"

"And this is a big story." The artificial sweetness disappeared.

"I don't know if there is a story." She didn't have time for this, and she sure didn't intend to tell Phil what she did know.

His voice grew serious. "Ivy, don't bullshit me, we've known each other too long. Jorge was my friend too, and I know about the dead Stater so don't play dumb. Way too many bodies to call it coincidence. I smell serial killer, and no matter what you say, or don't say, I'm running with the story. The people have the right to know."

Ivy sighed. On one level, she understood, yet the law-enforcement side of her wanted to duct-tape Phil's mouth. After serial killers Gary Ridgeway in Seattle and Robert Yates in Spokane terrorized the east and the west sides of the state, the last thing Moses Lake needed was to panic over the possibility that another one had made a home in their town.

"I honestly can't confirm, Phil, and that's not bullshit."

"Ivy, come on, we're old friends." He tried the pleading voice now.

"Yes, we are, and I'm telling you straight up, I can't confirm it's the work of a serial killer. Look, I'm on my way to Spokane right now. Let me see what I find out. Keep the serial-killer theory to yourself for twenty-four hours as a favor to your old pal, and I promise to make you my first call when I have more concrete information."

"You swear?" He didn't sound convinced, not that she blamed him. Despite all the years they'd known each other, they were on vastly different sides of the story. Law and media didn't mix well most of the time.

"Cross my heart and hope to die." *Please let it go.*

"Okay, Hernandez, I'll hold you to that."

"Thanks."

She breathed in relief as she snapped the phone shut. Wheedling a twenty-four-hour reprieve from Phil was big, but she and Riah had better come up with a good story for him or they'd have even more problems. Phil knew lots of people with really powerful pens, and he could stir things up fast. Also, she didn't want people in her hometown to be afraid. Moses Lake might not be the prettiest town in the state, but it was home. It deserved to be left in peace.

Ivy took a sip of her latte and let it warm her. As she drove, she managed to put Phil out of her mind and instead tried to talk herself into being not pissed off about the state trooper. The coroner for Adams County was a lawyer. The prosecuting attorney, no less. Though he filled the shoes of the coroner, unlike Ivy, he wasn't a doctor and didn't do autopsies. Victims came to either Moses Lake or Spokane under a mutual-cooperation agreement between the counties. In this instance, he requested Riah's assistance rather than Ivy's.

Until recently, they came to her in Moses Lake. Adams County didn't have many suspicious deaths, and because of the light workload in Moses Lake she was better able to handle them. Spokane was much busier and typically only took them from Adams County when something unusual occurred or Ivy's department was unable to assist. That scenario had happened only once since Ivy became coroner.

Ivy would be insulted as well as pissed off that Ned hadn't called except she knew why. After her divorce from Jorge, Ned hit on her hard. When she turned him down, he'd been pissed off. If Ned could have reined it in and waited a little longer to make his interest known, she might have taken him up on the offer. He was a good-looking guy, as well as smart and successful. But his timing sucked, and when she told him no, he acted like a spoiled little boy. His unflattering antics pretty much screwed up any chance he might have had, and these days he treated her as if she didn't exist. He'd call her for help if, and only if, he had no other option.

So Riah now had the body of the murdered trooper in her cooler, and Ivy knew about this death only because Riah kept her in the loop. It'd be fun to see the look on Ned's face if he found out she was on her way to assist with the autopsy he'd tried to exclude her from.

In the big picture, Ned didn't rate much consideration. His petty behavior was precisely that…petty. If Destiny held true to the pattern she'd established so far, the trooper would make his transition from death to undeath in about two hours.

What kind of game was Destiny playing? Vampires didn't always leave their victims in a state where they were guaranteed to turn. They could kill them for food and leave them good old-fashioned dead. Just because they died at the hands of a vampire, they wouldn't automatically turn. The vampire made the choice.

For a long time, Riah didn't share with Ivy what made the difference between food or follower. It all centered on trust. It took a while, but when Riah finally realized she could trust Ivy unconditionally, she opened up about her long existence in the shadows.

The secret between death and undeath had to do with blood, Riah had explained. Ivy remembered thinking *duh*. Every person who ever watched a movie, read a book, or researched folk legends understood vampires were all about the blood of their victims. But it wasn't as simple as Ivy thought.

Blood had to be shared for undeath to come knocking. Riah had been turned when the vampire's blood mixed with her own. Just a bite alone wasn't enough to turn a human into a creature of the night. One drop of the vampire's blood ingested by a victim, however, was. Whether by mouth or through the bloodstream, a drop made the difference.

It wasn't just turning a victim though. Vampires were supposed to follow unwritten rules. If a vampire turned a victim, they became that victim's master. They taught them how to survive, they cared for them, they never abandoned them. They were their maker, their teacher, their protector.

Destiny wasn't just taking victims for food. She was playing a very dangerous game and only she knew the rules. Each victim so far had turned, which meant she fed them her own blood, then turned around and discarded them like trash. What she was doing went against everything Riah had explained.

All the way to Spokane, Ivy kept thinking one thing—why?

CHAPTER THIRTEEN

Night fell quiet and dark. Destiny rose and stretched like a cat. Tonight promised all manner of fun except, first, she needed to feed. She took a shower, dried her long blond hair, and dressed. Black jeans, a bloodred blouse topped by a black jacket, and a nice pair of leather boots, handmade in Italy. Casual yet elegant. Striking enough to catch the attention of a willing victim while subdued enough not to stand out. Nobody had to tell her how good she looked.

The lights from Riverpark Square shone bright and cheerful. Saturday night was in full swing and she was just one of the crowd. Couples walked arm-in-arm while hordes of teenagers rode the escalators in the Square up to the third-floor multiplex.

At a wine bar on Howard, she found a nice table where she sat and twirled a long-stemmed goblet half full of an aromatic red. This seemed to be a popular hangout, exactly what she had in mind. The wine was excellent, though it didn't quench her thirst.

She didn't have to wait long, not that she ever did. As far back as she could remember, both before and after coming over, she'd drawn admirers wherever she went. It was a gift and a curse, her special brand of allure that took her from death to undeath.

The one who'd found her alongside the dark muddy road had been as ugly as Destiny was beautiful. That night, she'd hovered a mere breath away from death. Then as life began to flow out of her body, his blood trickled bitter and hot between her lips. She still recalled the peace of that moment.

What her life became afterward was nothing she could have imagined. It was beautiful and horrifying. Before, her life revolved around pleasure and the pursuit of wealth. After, pleasure and wealth were still important. So too were power and revenge.

"Hi," the man said, interrupting her reverie.

Destiny looked up and smiled. Not bad. Tall and dark-haired with a fashionable beard and mustache. His black slacks were stylish and expensive. So, too, was the gray shirt. "Hello," she said.

"Are you waiting for someone?" His eyes were rich chocolate brown.

"No." She ran her tongue over her lower lip. "Would you care to join me?"

He smiled and his eyes seemed to light up. "I'd love to."

"Are you here alone?" Why would such a tasty treat be out alone on a Saturday night? Destiny could smell the sweetness of his blood, hear the pulse of it as it coursed through his veins.

He looked sheepish. "Yes. I live across the street in the River Ridge condos. Every once in a while when I'm feeling cooped up I come over here. This place has the best wines in town. By the way, I'm Dale." He held out a hand.

She took the offered hand and shook it. "Destiny." He had a broad palm and long fingers that wrapped around hers. His nails were clean, manicured.

Much later, she stood looking out the tall windows of Dale's tasteful condo. As they'd walked from the wine bar, he'd promised the view was killer. He hadn't exaggerated. From his front room, the sight of the Spokane Falls was breathtaking. Floodlights bathed the falls in white light, the raw power of the water more than impressive as it roared between the basalt cliffs.

Destiny watched for a few minutes longer, then sighed. It was time to go. She walked back to the bedroom and began to pick up her clothes. Dale had proved to be an energetic and enthusiastic lover. She'd thoroughly enjoyed herself. The little romp had filled her with energy. The blood didn't hurt either. It was a lovely way to start a long and eventful night.

Once dressed, she stopped in the bedroom doorway and glanced back. Dale was stretched across the bed, his eyes closed and his skin pale in the darkened room. He appeared to be deep in sleep, if one didn't look too closely.

❖

Colin glanced at his watch. Jesus, it was already almost ten. He shoved up from the hotel bed and headed for the shower. He couldn't believe he'd slept that long. Then again, Ivy had done her best to wear him out. He smiled. God help him, he'd take that kind of workout any day of the week. Beat the heck out of going to the hotel gym.

He rested his head against the shower enclosure and closed his eyes, letting warm water flow down his back. It was stupid to get sidetracked. He had no business jumping into bed with anyone, especially in the middle of a hunt like this one. Then again...

Love at first sight wasn't something Colin believed in. It was hormones. It was an itch. It was anything except love, because love at first sight didn't exist. Of course, most people would swear vampires didn't exist either.

Still, he told himself he wasn't in love with the dark-haired beauty. The notion was ridiculous. He might be in lust—he'd buy that. Love—not a chance. Except from the first second he touched her, something was very different. And not in a bad way different.

Love wasn't exactly something Colin had much experience with. Sure, he'd started life as a loved and wanted child. His parents had been the best and all his memories were good. Having that foundation was probably the only thing that kept him from crashing into madness.

Once his family was gone, all he had were his memories. Monsignor did his best to fill the void left by the loss of his family, and he did the job well, all things considered.

Still, it wasn't the same. The monsignor gave him the unconditional love of a family while at the same time molding him into the hunter he ultimately became. It wasn't exactly a normal upbringing. He was always the guy on the outside, just a step out of touch with all the others. Most of the time, it was fine. He understood who he was and why. Then, there were times when Colin wanted to be like everyone else—oblivious to the dangers lurking in the shadows of the night. To be able to go to college, chase women, and drink beer. Just a regular Joe Blow.

What he wanted and what he was were two very different things. The night his family was destroyed took the possibility of choice from him. So, when he wished to be like everyone else, when he wanted nothing more than to be a regular guy, he pushed the desires away and concentrated on what he was—a vampire hunter.

Now, after all this time, the end was in sight. It both thrilled and scared him. Without a concrete goal, what would his life become? He'd never considered what he would do once he cleansed the earth of vampires. It was the only thing he knew how to do.

He immediately thought of Ivy. Was she God's gift to him? Was she the pot of gold at the end of the rainbow? Or, was he seeing things in her that didn't exist because he was scared?

Colin pulled his head up and let the water hit him in the face. It didn't really matter one way or the other. Life would be what life would be. He had to focus on one thing—destroying the last two vampires on the planet.

By the time he was dressed and in his car, he felt more like himself. Steady, focused. No more thoughts of love. He picked up his cell phone and called Ivy. The moment he heard her voice, a rush went right up his spine. Yeah…fling.

"Colin." His name rolled off her tongue like honey. "I'm glad you called."

"Are you all right?" Though her voice sounded sweet, he had the feeling something wasn't right.

"I'm on my way to Spokane."

"Why?" His thoughts shifted into hunter mode.

"She took out a state trooper last night."

"Where?" He did have a broad vocabulary, but as his mind raced, everything seemed to come out in single syllables.

"Sprague Lake. It's between Spokane and Moses Lake. I'm on my way now to meet Riah and Adriana at the morgue."

"How far out are you?"

"Just pulled off I-90 onto Maple. I'll be there in about five minutes."

"I'll meet you there, I'm close as well."

He snapped the phone shut and concentrated on traffic. At first he was surprised at the amount of it until he remembered it was Saturday. He hated Saturdays. For him it wasn't a night to party. No, for Colin, Saturday night was the busiest night of the week.

At the Public Safety Building, he found a parking spot near the rear entrance of the morgue. He glanced up in time to see Ivy turn off Broadway in the direction of the security gate. He waved. She saw him and stopped long enough for him to jump into the passenger's seat.

"Good timing," he said.

She smiled and pulled into a parking spot after the guard cleared them through the gate. Once the car was turned off, she didn't move. "You didn't wake me." She spoke very quietly.

Colin wasn't sure what he heard in her voice. "You needed the sleep." It was lame.

Ivy shifted so her dark gaze fell on his face. The dashboard lights made the inside of the car glow enough he could see her expression. "You could have said good-bye."

He might as well 'fess up even if it did make him sound like a scared little boy. "I was too chicken to wake you up."

Ivy's laugh was gentle, forgiving.

She grabbed his hand. "Amen."

His shoulders relaxed—a little. There was still the issue of his destroying her friend, but he'd cross that bridge later. "You too?"

"You know it. I'm just not the kind of girl who jumps in bed with every vampire hunter she runs into."

"You run into a lot of vampire hunters?" God, he liked the feel of her hand in his.

"Oh, yes, at least one every week."

He loved the way her eyes danced. "You're full of it."

This time she really laughed and leaned over to kiss him. "It's a definite possibility."

He ran his tongue across her lower lip as he entwined his hand in her dark, lush hair. He pulled her a little closer to kiss her deeper.

She tasted wonderful and smelled like heaven. He didn't want to think about leaving her.

"What is it about you?" he asked against her lips.

"I could ask you the same thing."

Colin gazed into her eyes and felt a twinge in his heart. Impossible. "You know this is crazy."

"Certifiable," she said.

"So, what are we going to do about it?"

Ivy pulled away and shrugged. "Right now, we're going to join the others, try to figure out what's happening, and then," she shrugged again, "who knows."

She was right. At the moment, the only thing they should be focused on was Destiny and the bloody trail she was leaving across the state. At least now they had a clue where she seemed to be heading.

He kissed Ivy one more time, then got out of the car. Night was burning and they were still a long way from any answers.

❖

"It's about damn time," Riah grumbled when Ivy and Colin pushed through the doors.

Ivy's eyes narrowed. "And hello to you too."

Ivy's response didn't surprise Riah. She'd never bought into Riah's moods, which were typically far more mercurial than Ivy's. Riah learned to trust Ivy partially because of her steadfast personality and her even temper. Ivy had a cool head no matter how out of control things became.

Except now. Riah wasn't blind. Ivy and Colin walked a little too close together and seemed to make a little too much effort not to look at each other. They'd slept together somewhere between the time they left here last night and now. She could almost smell it on them.

Ivy might think the tall, cool vampire hunter was a hot piece of ass, but Riah? Not so much. Oh, he was attractive enough and the kind of man women noticed even if they weren't inclined toward the opposite sex. Something about him was different and alluring.

He was also tough and smart. Nothing soft about this hunter. All the more reason to question putting complete trust in him. Riah hadn't lived nearly five hundred years through random or naïve trust. She'd have been destroyed a very long time ago if she had.

Though Ivy was a mere human, this was likewise far out of character for her. Particularly with Destiny's recent choice of Jorge as a victim thrown into the mix.

Something truly evil was headed her way and she had no idea why. She'd kept her promise to do no harm these last few centuries. She even became a physician, Hippocratic Oath and all. She'd stayed true to her oath and her promise. Riah helped the dead to speak. Her science put away murderers and monsters. She comforted families and tried to make amends for past sins. She hadn't once in over two hundred years taken a human life.

Perhaps in the last two centuries, she'd become too complacent. Perhaps evil had stalked her for years and she'd been too involved trying to atone for her past to see the signs. Certainly, she missed the passing of so many like herself. Years ago, she'd have known immediately when another vampire was destroyed. Their culture was close-knit. But she'd walked away from her life as well as those she'd previously called her friends. Most viewed her choice as betrayal. From the day she'd been turned, she'd been an outcast in human society, and when she'd turned her back on the vampire world, she'd become an outcast there too.

Now, both of her worlds were about to collide and she didn't understand why. All she knew was in some strange way she was involved. If she didn't come up with answers soon, all of Adriana's work would be for naught. Riah wouldn't be here long enough for the cure to matter.

She pulled herself away from her disturbing thoughts and turned her attention to the cooler where the body of the state trooper chilled. She left the other three talking in low voices and pulled the cooler door open. A whoosh of cold air hit her in the face, the scent of decay and destruction wafting out. She shivered.

Sunset had come and gone with nary a twitch beneath the body bag. So far, it seemed Destiny played with her food, then left them to turn as the next night fell. Through the years, Riah had seen it a hundred times or more. Vamps who were bored or lonely, turning their victims in the hope that having someone by their side could make them feel excited or even loved. Most of the unfortunate victims never made it past a sunset or two.

The life of a vampire wasn't easy or glamorous, despite the picture the popular media presented. It was cold, lonely, and ugly. Not once in all her years did Riah try to turn another. She lacked the courage to end her own existence, but she couldn't bring another into the shadows. She refused to become what Rodolphe always hoped he could mold her into.

Destiny was an enigma. She turned each victim yet she didn't seem to do it for sport or companionship. Not when she threw them aside like trash. It didn't make sense. Nor did this most recent victim. She drained the trooper and tossed him away. The trooper was good and dead. So, why the shift after she left so many to turn?

Riah pushed him out of the cooler, the wheels sounding a steady squeak, squeak, squeak as the gurney rolled toward the autopsy room. She positioned him beneath the high-powered light and turned it until it shone on his face. His cheeks were sunken, his skin pasty. His eyes were smoky, reminding her of an old dog slowly going blind. What had made him interesting and special was gone.

"He's not moving," Adriana commented, her head tilted, her dark eyes narrowed.

"No," Riah answered. "She didn't try to turn him."

All four of them stood around the gurney now, staring down at the dead man. Riah had all her implements laid out and ready. She didn't move to pick up a single tool.

"I don't get it," Ivy said. "Why not?"

Riah crossed her arms as she lifted her gaze to Colin's face. "Do you know?"

His eyes narrowed as he returned her steady scrutiny. "I can only guess."

"Guess away."

CHAPTER FOURTEEN

Destiny could smell her before the door even opened. When it did, she smiled as she stood under the cover of darkness. Despite all the years, she still recalled every detail about the woman now called Dr. Riah Preston. The years had changed little. The harsh light of the delivery area did nothing to dampen her beauty. Her long dark hair, held back in a clip, was as thick and silky as ever. Beneath the shapeless blue scrubs was a spectacular body with slim hips and firm breasts.

A chill raced up her back as another woman stepped out of the door Riah held open. She too was a petite beauty with skin as dark as Riah's was pale. Her fingers brushed Riah's cheek as she stepped into the light. Destiny smiled and licked her lips. Some things never changed, even after half a millennium.

The two women walked to a compact car parked in the shadows across from the door. They walked close, their bodies touching in a way only those who are intimate can. Lovers.

If she had any doubt of her assessment, it was laid to rest when the two embraced and kissed for a very long moment. Then Riah's lover got in the car and began to back it out of the parking spot.

Destiny wasted no time, but sprinted to her car parked on the street outside the gates. By the time the woman pulled out onto Broadway, Destiny was right behind her. It was easy to keep her in sight.

Ten minutes later, when the woman's car pulled into the garage of a lovely home, Destiny was tempted to follow her inside and enlighten the woman on the true nature of her beloved. She resisted temptation and parked a discreet distance away. Keeping to the shadows, she studied the house. With the blinds drawn, the windows in front were useless. The rear was better. Because the back of the house overlooked the bluff, apparently the woman didn't feel the need to cover the windows.

The woman stripped out of her clothes. Lover-girl was a tasty little morsel and arousal surged. It wasn't hard to figure out what Riah saw in this woman. She'd love to take a few minutes and see what kind of music they could make together.

As she watched, the woman slipped on a light robe, then went to the case she'd brought with her from the ME's office. She picked it up and left the bedroom. Destiny managed to get to the kitchen window in time to see her head down to a basement. It was fortunate this little beauty turned out to be a good homeowner. Egress windows into the basement provided a clear view of a lab setup. What exactly were Riah and her lover up to? She watched for about five minutes before returning to her car.

In good time, she'd be back.

"Don't drive to Moses Lake," Colin had said to her in the parking lot. Common sense told Ivy to drive her little butt right back home. What happened last night was a one-time thing, right? Impulsive and wonderful, but nothing that should happen again. Except, instead of heading south on Monroe to hit the I-90 on-ramp, she was pulling into the parking lot of the hotel right behind Colin. Her hands shook as she gripped the steering wheel.

Then again, it was Saturday night, or rather Sunday morning. No one waited for her at home. No one needed her back in Grant County so why not have a little fun? Or, a little more fun.

Colin was at her car door by the time she slipped the car into Park. In the darkness of the early morning hours, he looked dangerous and sexy. It struck Ivy how different he was from Jorge. The sudden thought of her dead ex-husband sent a little shiver up her spine. She'd wanted Jorge to let go of the past and move on. Yet, never did she consider the possibility her freedom might come on the heels of death.

The price was too high. She didn't want to be free of Jorge at such a cost. In her mind, it meant nothing more than him moving on and finding someone more suitable. The choice hadn't been hers to make. Someone else made it for them. Jorge was dead. She didn't like the way it happened nor could she change it.

Ivy opened the door, swung her feet out of the car, and took the hand Colin offered. His fingers wrapped around hers, warm and comforting. With her free hand, she held the key fob out, pushed the small red button, and listened for the click and beep.

He kissed her lightly. "What is it about you?" he whispered against her lips.

"What is it about me?" Ivy tilted her head to see his face a little better.

"I'm here to hunt an old and devious vampire, yet all I can think about is you."

She studied his face. He wasn't smiling. "You are distracted by me, aren't you?"

He walked with her inside the bright lobby of the hotel. Following the hallway to the bank of elevators, he waited until they were alone and ascending. Her back was against the wall and he faced her, both hands on the wall over her head.

"You distract me more than is healthy for either of us." His green eyes were serious.

"I'm sorry." Maybe she should drive back to Moses Lake. It'd probably be the wisest thing to do. She tried not to think about how fabulous he smelled or how she wanted to run her hands up his chest.

"I'm not."

"But you said..." She tilted her head and stared into his face.

"Yeah." He ran a hand through his hair, making it stand on end as if he just came in from a strong windstorm. He turned until his back was also against the elevator wall. "I've been at this a long time. I've done things that, if I really stopped to think about them, would probably send me over the edge."

The haunting echo in his voice made her take his hand. She hated to think about what his life was like. She dealt in death every day, though, by and large, hers was a world where mysteries unraveled and answers provided peace to distraught families. With, of course, occasional exceptions, like Jorge.

Exceptions aside, her world had a normalcy that didn't exist for Colin. Death touched his daily life just as it did for Ivy, but nothing in his confrontation with death could be characterized as normal. Everything that flowed in and around him was a touch outside reality. How he managed to stay sane was nothing short of a miracle.

"I'm glad you haven't tipped over that edge," she told him, and rested her head against his shoulder.

The doors of the elevator slid open and Colin pulled her into the hallway, holding her. They passed half a dozen doors before he stopped and slipped the cardkey into a door. A green light glowed just above the door handle and Colin opened the door. He released his grip on her and she walked into the cool interior of the room. Her entire body buzzed.

Colin flipped the light switch in the bathroom and the gold light filtered out to the main room. She kept her back to him. The only thing she really noticed was the inviting king-sized bed. A gentle silence fell over the room.

Ivy turned when the long silence stretched. Colin leaned against the bathroom doorframe with his arms crossed and his gaze fixed on her. She loved the way his hair curled around the collar of his jacket and a five o'clock shadow darkened his jaw. His jeans were just snug enough to be sexy without looking lounge-lizard tight. A button-down black cotton shirt was casual despite a muscled chest with a sprinkling of curly hair beneath.

Her heart beat quickened, her pulse raced. When was the last time she felt this alive? Or this horny? Never. Not even with Jorge and she'd married him. Right now, it was taking every bit of self-control she possessed not to race over and rip the clothes off him.

Ivy's world had taken a shift to the left when Riah came clean and introduced her to the shady and relatively secret world of vampires. Nothing had been quite the same since. Now, her life was shifting yet again, this time courtesy of a vampire hunter. It was getting harder to remember what normal looked like.

"So…" he drawled. "What now?"

Ivy licked her lips. "I thought you had a plan."

He raised an eyebrow. "Hungry? It's not too late for room service."

She studied his face as she shook her head and frowned. "Not hungry."

"Tired?"

This time she smiled. Okay, she saw how this was going down. Game. Set. Match. "Not even a little."

She began to unbutton her shirt.

❖

After everyone left and Riah was alone in the autopsy room, she sat on a stool just staring at the cooler door. Everything was cleaned up and the trooper was back on ice, so to speak. The funeral home would pick him up tomorrow. The autopsy, though completed rather quickly compared to normal circumstances, was nothing special other than the fact he'd been drained of blood.

One of Riah's well-practiced skills as a medical examiner was the ability to document a vampire death as something different than it really was. The trooper's death certificate would list nothing even close to the reality of his preternaturally hastened demise. The devil was in the details and Riah's details would spin a very different story. Everyone was infinitely happier with an explanation they could make sense of.

It wasn't the death certificate that had her thinking now, but the conversation with the vampire hunter that sent her thoughts racing at warp speed. Despite her reservations about Colin, he made some very interesting points. Perhaps *interesting* was the wrong word. More like disturbing.

Riah wanted to dislike the hunter who was as mysterious as he was handsome. Ivy was obviously entranced, almost as if he was preternatural himself and had used a bit of glimmer to lure the gorgeous Ivy into his bed. Riah recognized others of darkness when she met them, and Colin was as human as Ivy. And as likeable as Ivy—damn him.

Riah didn't routinely indulge in stupidity, and she'd be stupid to blindly trust this man. It wasn't about trust; it was gut instinct. Plain, old-fashioned honesty oozed from his pores. It was probably one of the things that made him a successful hunter. Few lasted more than a couple years in his chosen profession, yet this man had made it the better part of a lifetime without finding himself a victim of the creatures he hunted.

His theories on the elusive Destiny bothered Riah. He obviously believed Destiny was fucking with her, and she wasn't inclined to argue the point. Everything seemed to support it. But why?

The state trooper, the only one Destiny didn't try to turn, must have been a necessary meal. Destiny was working on maintaining full power, and a strong, virile man—like a Washington State Patrolman—was the perfect ticket. It was only a theory, though, and she hoped they were right.

At the same time, Riah wondered if a clock was ticking somewhere in the background. And if it was, how much time was left?

"Hey, Doc?"

Riah looked up to see Andrew in the doorway. "Hi, A.J."

"Everything okay with you? I saw some other folks in here on my last round."

She nodded. "Things are fine and everyone else has left. It's just me now."

He narrowed his eyes and seemed to study her face. "You sure everything's okay? I don't mean to be rude, Doc, but you look a little...I don't know...not like yourself."

She didn't feel like herself either. "I'm just thinking about a case."

"Well, if you're sure. I can take a look around if you want."

"I'm okay, I promise."

He stayed in the doorway, his eyes still narrow and appraising. Then his face seemed to clear and he shrugged. "Okay then. I'm here until six if you need me."

She nodded. "Thanks, A.J. I'll be heading out shortly anyway."

"Why don't you let me walk you to the car?"

She smiled at the former navy man who was so very serious about his current job. "I'll be fine."

"Hey, Doc…" He didn't return her smile. His hand was again resting on the butt of his gun.

"Yes?"

"Humor me."

CHAPTER FIFTEEN

It took less than twenty minutes for Destiny to return to the Public Safety Building. Had to love the lack of traffic in this place. Too bad she couldn't stay longer. Behind the gates that shielded the staff from the general public, the cars had thinned since her earlier visit. Only one remained.

Destiny watched for about an hour before Riah came out the door. Artificial light rained down harsh on her pale skin. By any standards, old or new, she was striking. That she hadn't aged a day didn't hurt either. Even so, the years had done something to her. It took Destiny a few moments of studying her face before she realized what it was. Riah was infinitely more beautiful now, as if time and knowledge gifted her with the only thing it could. Maturity in heart and soul made her even more alluring.

It was difficult to hold onto restraint. Destiny ached to reveal herself to Riah, to confront the woman who'd haunted her dreams. She wanted to touch her firm breasts, kiss her full lips…wrap her fingers around her throat.

She didn't. Not yet.

Instead, she watched while Riah chatted with the handsome security guard before getting into her car and driving into the night. This time, Destiny didn't follow Riah as she'd done earlier with the other woman. She watched until the taillights of her car were long gone.

Now, it was simply a matter of patience. She might not like having to wait, but after the many years already, one more night was nothing. The reality was, in twenty-four hours, the long-awaited vengeance would be hers.

Destiny smiled, unbuttoned the top three buttons of her sweater, and put a hand beneath each breast, adjusting them until they almost spilled out of her sweater. Once the man turned his back to where Destiny stood and began to walk in the opposite direction, she leapt over the fence. Her movements were silent as she landed inside the secure area. Her long hair fluttered before settling around her shoulders in a golden cloud.

"Excuse me, ma'am." He must have sensed her and now turned toward her, a flashlight shining on her face. His brow wrinkled and his eyes narrowed. One hand drifted to the gun at his waist. "What're you doing here?"

She smiled into the directed light, a hand over her eyes. Her tongue slid slowly over her bottom lip. "Looking for you."

He lowered the light so it no longer blinded her. His hand didn't move from the gun. "Do I know you?"

He was very attractive—for a human. She broadened her smile enough that her lengthening canines were visible, pearl-white and glistening in the inky night. "Not yet, but you will."

She covered the distance between them in less than a second. The flashlight clattered to the asphalt, the light whirling across the black parking lot like a carnival spotlight. His hand was no longer on the gun.

❖

For a moment, Colin stood frozen in the bathroom doorway. Ivy's hands captured his attention as they moved from button to button, the fabric of her shirt falling away to reveal her full breasts. Her bra was pale pink, which wasn't a color he'd have associated with a woman who made her living amongst the dead. Black, yeah— pink, never. But, he liked it…a lot.

Her shirt fell with a swish to the floor. Her pants followed. In her bra and panties, she made his blood rush straight to his cock, finally propelling him into motion. He drew her against his body and covered her lips with his. His tongue demanded as he cupped her ass, pulling her tight against his hard-on.

She smelled as good as she tasted. Her scent was light, easy, as if she'd just stepped in from a fresh spring rain. He could spend the rest of his life holding this woman and inhaling the wonderful scent unique to her, especially if she was naked.

The rest of his life? The thought was extreme enough he almost stepped away from her. Yeah, that was gonna happen. This whole hunt had him off his game in more ways than one. They were just going to fuck, right? None of this make-love crap. Not his style. Until now. It was impossible to even convince himself this was just a casual hookup.

He used his lips to trace a line down her neck to the swell of her breasts, concentrating on nothing but the taste and feel of Ivy. Thank God, he'd checked into a decent hotel instead of some dive on the edge of town, as he was often prone to do. Maybe God really did have a hand in this.

Ivy pulled his belt free and tossed it aside. It landed on the floor with a thud. She had his pants unbuttoned, unzipped, and at his ankles so fast it barely registered in his foggy brain.

"Oh, naked," she murmured, her breath hot against the bare skin of his thighs. "I love a man daring enough to bare it underneath his jeans." She kissed the hot skin of his hip.

With her face mere inches from his cock, it throbbed hard. "Less laundry," he whispered back, his voice strangled.

Her light laugh distracted him for a moment. At least until she dipped her head and licked the tip of his cock while her hands moved to his feet. His concentration was shot. The touch of her tongue against his hot tip made him shudder all over. Her hands pushed at his shoes, and within a few seconds they were off, along with his pants. Her tongue continued to stroke the length of him while her hands moved up his legs to his butt and beneath the shirt he still wore.

Then her lips closed over his cock and he shuddered all over. Eyes shut, his hands in her hair, he felt his control slipping. Everything tightened and he was afraid he'd come right now.

He was surprised when she stopped. Slowly, she slid her hands up his body until they stood together. She kissed his nipples, his neck, then his lips.

"Still want dinner?" she whispered.

Laughing, he pulled her to the bed. He pushed her down, then covered her body with his. "Oh, I'm hungry all right."

"For?"

"I think you know."

Colin held her hands above her head and kissed her neck before turning his attention to her perfect breasts. She wiggled beneath him and struggled to free her hands.

"You know I have you captive," he said when he raised his head while he still held her hands immobile. "I'm a big tough vampire hunter, remember?"

She smiled and raised her eyebrows. "You weren't so tough a minute ago."

"Touché."

He released her hands and continued kissing down her body until he reached the patch of dark curly hair. It was time to make her squirm. He licked her clit and she bucked against him. Her moans encouraged him and he licked her again. Her fingers snaked into his hair. A little more full attention was just what she needed, and he slipped two fingers inside. She was hot, very wet, and her back arched.

"Oh, my God," she whimpered. "You're killing me."

He pressed a kiss against the inside of her thigh. "But it'll be a sweet death."

"I'll get even," she said breathlessly.

"Promise?"

He moved his fingers inside her and she bucked against his hand. "Oh, yeah."

When he sensed she was ready to explode, he slipped his fingers out and moved up to kiss her lips. As he gazed down into her dark eyes, he felt something he'd never experienced before. He loved Ivy

Hernandez, and it didn't matter that it went against everything he believed in.

"You're so beautiful," he murmured.

She let out a sigh and grabbed his ass with both hands. "Enough with the small talk, mister big, bad vampire hunter. Time to put out."

With a smile, he entered her. He moved against her, in and out, faster and faster. Her moans mingled with his, and when he came, the explosion shook him to his soul.

Afterward, he lay next to her, holding her close with his heart pounding. He kissed the top of her head and thought love had to be about the greatest thing in the world.

Riah drove toward Adriana's. The house was dark and the streets deserted, past time for decent people to be in. In fact, it was just about time for decent people to be crawling out of bed and preparing for the new day. Riah kept going and barely slowed in front of the house.

It had been so many years since Riah truly loved another, and now her emotions were all over the board. Adriana managed to touch a part of her dormant for some five centuries, give or take. All that time, Riah'd done quite nicely without feeling anything for another, particularly a mortal. Her friends and lovers, for the most part, had been other vampires. It was safer, both physically and emotionally.

Of course, when she'd come to this country, things changed. She'd learned to trust humans because she'd had little choice. It was either trust them or fail. Many along the way surprised her with their capacity for understanding and willingness to be her friend despite her past.

People like Ivy and Adriana. It was fine and good when it was simply a matter of dealing with trust and friendship. Adriana had pushed the stakes up a notch. The last thing Riah ever thought she'd find herself faced with again was love.

She idled down the boulevard, the lights of her car cutting through the slight fog rising from the river below. She liked this time just before the world rose. Unlike most, she moved between daylight and shadow with relative ease. It left her alone during hours like these when the creatures of the night returned to the shadows. Despite the urge to do otherwise, she drove past Adriana's house.

Once home, she strolled down the hall to her bedroom and stripped, leaving her clothes on the floor where they fell. After showering, she slipped into a silk robe and went to the small cooler. It was necessary to feed even when it was the last thing she felt like doing. As she drank, she gazed up. In the portrait, a ruby pendant glistened around Meriel's neck. The intricate gold work was magnificent, and Riah smiled, remembering the night she'd given it to her lover.

Jonathan Verian was a master craftsman much sought out in their elite social circle. It took some doing, but Riah managed to sweet-talk him into creating the beautiful trinket. The look on Meriel's face the night Riah gave her the necklace was worth all the effort it took to get it made.

Riah turned away from the portrait, chills sliding up her back as she recalled the last time she'd seen the necklace. Beautiful was the last thing it had been at that awful moment. She closed her eyes and envisioned it as clearly as if she was standing right there. It didn't sparkle in the moonlight because it was smeared with crimson blood and tangled around the neck of Meriel's cold, lifeless body.

She pushed the memory away and walked to her bed, only to stand and stare at it. Rest was impossible. After a full minute of doing nothing, Riah turned away from the big bed and went to her bag. She pulled out the copy of Colin's map she'd made at the office. Spreading it out flat on her desk, she clicked on the lamp. Light spilled down, making the marks and notes come into clear focus. In fact, they seemed to jump off the page.

Ivy was right. Whoever this Destiny was, she was making serious tracks toward Riah. It still rubbed her wrong because she didn't know this vampire. It also didn't help that Colin and his cronies had managed to wipe out nearly the entire vampire community. In some respects their success should make it easier for Riah to figure it out. It didn't. Destiny was completely off the radar.

When her computer booted up, Riah logged on to her secure ME site. She glanced at the first location Colin marked, then plugged in the name of the city and waited while the search engine did its work. Thank God for the Internet. A few seconds later, she hit pay dirt. An hour later, Riah managed to successfully search each location noted on the map.

Her notes in order, she laid down her pen and pushed back in her chair. "Sweet Jesus," she muttered.

❖

Colin stood at the window while Ivy slept peacefully in the bed, her dark hair spread out on the pillow. She was so gorgeous. She looked good in clothes, but naked—she made him hard all over again. It wouldn't take too much to make him jump right back into bed. Except she needed her sleep and he needed something else.

He turned his attention back to the window. His cell phone rested in the palm of his hand, the ringer turned to vibrate. In the last half hour, the wind had kicked up and the trees around the hotel bent and swayed. A storm was on its way.

Almost an hour had passed since he crawled out of the warm bed, and the wait seemed interminable. When was the damn phone going to ring? Things were rapidly getting out of control. He wasn't so much concerned about taking down Destiny. Quite the opposite, in fact; he was locked, loaded, and ready for bear. The anticipation of destroying a bloodthirsty vampire wasn't what had him feeling so twitchy.

It was two things. Or, to be more accurate, two women: Ivy and Riah.

Woman number one was completely unexpected. Ivy made his blood pound and his heart soar. Though he was always in control, the minute she touched him, he was a goner. Never in his wildest imagination could he have seen this coming.

But it was happening way too fast. He knew what it took to win in battle against the creatures of darkness. The formula was very simple. Two critical elements: patience and time. Worked for him every time—at least as far as vampires were concerned.

This thing with Ivy was neither patient nor slow. It was hot, fast, and all-consuming. It went against everything he was and everything he believed. On those rare occasions when he did let his body rule, he still didn't jump in bed with women he barely knew. It was all about satisfying a need without emotion entering into the mix. He understood it; the women he slept with understood it. No one was hurt and everyone walked away satisfied while still friends. More of a friends-with-benefits kind of thing.

With Ivy, it went beyond a friendly encounter. The two of them were neck deep in passion while he was supposed to be concentrating on keeping the world safe. Hunting and sex simply didn't mix. Not once in all his years had he allowed himself to be preoccupied with sex when he was on a vampire's trail, and he sure never fell in love.

All his very workable and trusty philosophies went into the crapper the minute Ivy showed up. She was a dark-haired addiction he craved like any dedicated alcoholic. He thought about her all the time. He could smell her even when she wasn't there. He itched to touch her the second he saw her. But oddest of all, it wasn't entirely about sex either. Just to be with her was as important as being able to make love to her. He wasn't sure what to do about it either. He also wasn't sure he *wanted* to do anything about it.

If all that wasn't confusing enough, he had Riah to consider. The bottom line with her was crystal clear. It was his sworn duty to destroy her. She was a destructive creature of the night, an unholy affront to the world as he knew it. She and her kind had massacred his family. Vampires took away any chance he might have had for a normal life.

Instead of football games, dates, and dances, he spent his formative years learning to hunt. He'd dedicated his entire life to destroying that which had taken those most precious from him. And, until now, it'd been easy.

Now, things were muddy. It was bad enough that Riah and Ivy were close friends. He could probably work around that fact if he rationalized it for a good long while. But he *liked* Riah. She was smart, kind, and trying to accomplish something good in the world. She was everything that went against the nature of a vampire. Nothing had prepared him for this reaction.

How exactly, then, could he pull his sword and take her head? How exactly could he *not* pull his sword and take her head? His world was so much nicer when everything was black or white, good or evil. He didn't like shades of gray one little bit.

The phone in his hand vibrated. He glanced at Ivy, happy to see she still slept peacefully. Heading to the bathroom, he pulled the door shut and flipped the phone open.

"Yes," he said softly.

"We've uncovered some interesting information about your new friend."

He didn't know if he should be excited or afraid. "Go ahead, Monsignor."

When he snapped the phone shut some fifteen minutes later, he was even more conflicted. What Monsignor discovered made so much sense it made him wonder why it hadn't occurred to him earlier. At the same time, it complicated his life even more. He was struggling before the call, but now a full-out war raged in his mind. Either way he looked, it wouldn't be good and someone would get hurt.

A few days ago, his life was simple. Track down vampires. Kill vampires. Make the world safe for the humans who never even knew he was protecting them. *Simple* suddenly seemed to have taken a permanent flight out the window. Yeah, he was still in the track-down-vampire mode. He would still kill vampires...he just wasn't so sure he could kill *all* the vampires. It sucked, it really, really did.

CHAPTER SIXTEEN

Something was wrong. Riah bolted upright, then stilled. The house was silent, empty, and dark as a crypt. Did she hear something or simply sense it?

She stood and walked to the window. Despite her earlier anxiety and belief that rest would elude her, she'd managed to sleep through the day. Darkness was just beginning to shroud the world outside her window. Soon the streetlights would glow a dull orange, and a butter moon would crest the mountains. The trees swayed in the wind. She scanned the street and her yard. Nothing. Whatever awakened her wasn't an imminent threat. She turned away from the window, heading to the bathroom.

Beneath the dual showerheads, she let the water pour over her body. It did little to tame the vibrations racing from head to toe. It had been what, two…three hundred years since she'd felt this way. Certainly not since before Rodolphe's demise. There'd been bloody vampire wars in those days. Alliances built and destroyed. Lands conquered and loyal followers made. Power was the name of the game and she'd played it with the best of them. Rodolphe had been an extraordinary teacher.

Riah didn't miss any of it.

Oh, there were always vampires who wanted supremacy and control. Particularly the young ones. A vampire didn't exist as long as Riah without gaining a great deal of wisdom. Power could be intoxicating, but more often than not it was a death sentence even for the immortal. Someone stronger, hungrier was always coming up from behind.

Harmony and forgiveness became most important to Riah. Stepping far away from the drama and power plays of darkness gave her no regrets. She wanted no part of them.

Truthfully, the battles were far less dramatic in the twenty-first century than earlier. Even vampires after so many centuries managed to learn and ultimately embrace both diplomacy and discretion. Or so she believed until a couple of days ago. If what Colin told her was true, none of it mattered because, soon, there'd be no more vampires.

Delusions weren't her specialty. Colin wouldn't spare her life unless Adriana came up with a miracle cure. Adriana's heart was in the right place but time wasn't on their side.

Right now, though, waves of emotion flowed through Riah, the same sense of anticipation before she'd followed Rodolphe into battle. They were often victorious, taking what they wanted and destroying anyone that stood in their way. He'd given her in undeath what she couldn't possess in life—independence. Though tied to Rodolphe as her maker and lover, she'd still been infinitely freer than she'd ever been as a young woman in the sixteenth century. No biological father to gamble her away. No adoptive father to marry her off to some withered old nobleman.

When she'd destroyed Rodolphe, everything changed yet again. Total freedom was hers. She walked away from her old life without a second look back. For some the solitary existence was unthinkable. Not for her. She embraced it and survived. Why, then, did she feel as though her world was about to implode?

She dried off and went to the chest of drawers. As she started to reach for a clean set of scrubs, she paused. The light blue garments were folded and ready for her next shift at the ME's office. After a moment, she closed the drawer and turned to the closet. Inside she shoved aside jackets, shirts, and dresses. In the back was a set of clothes she'd been unable to part with even though she honestly believed she'd never need to wear them again.

The black leather pants fit as well tonight as the first day she'd slipped into them. The leather was smooth and warm against her naked skin. The tailor who'd made them was an Italian wizard. A smile tugged at the corners of her mouth as her mind turned back the years. Nothing she'd asked him for had been too strange or difficult, even if he did give her a few questioning looks.

The leather attire pleased her a great deal. Despite being born into privilege where dresses and beauty were highly prized, they were never really her forte. By the dawn of the American Revolution, dresses and convention no longer suited Riah. She moved alone in the shadows even back then and chose appropriate clothing.

Aiden Marcetti crafted the gorgeous black leather pants, vest, and ankle-length jacket hundreds of years before popular culture's spate of vampire anti-heroes made the look a part of folk legend. In the dark clothing, she moved undetected through the back alleys of the cities as well as through the shadows of the rural lands. She was no longer on the search for tasty prey. Instead, she was a silent and deadly hunter whose sole intent was to protect unsuspecting victims from others of her own kind. She did her good deeds in absolute anonymity.

From a box on the top shelf of the closet, Riah removed a silver dagger. She turned it over in her hands, reacquainting herself with the weight and feel of the weapon before she slid it into a sheath at her hip. Several silver throwing stars fit into invisible pockets inside her jacket. Finally, one more dagger, a bit longer than the one at her hip yet still shorter than a sword, slid into a sheath sewn into the lining of her jacket. It felt as familiar tonight as it did a couple of centuries ago.

Dressed and armed, Riah stilled and listened once more. Nothing but silence throughout her house. She shook her head and moved to the mirror. She wasn't imagining things and, though she might very well be alone in the house at the moment, somewhere very close, danger waited. Something was in the wind and it whispered to her.

❖

Ivy was alone. Again. The guy was like a ghost. No wonder he was a vampire hunter. Even the creatures of darkness with all their preternatural senses probably never heard him coming. With her strictly human senses, Ivy sure didn't hear him leave, either time.

Ivy rolled out of bed and headed to the shower. She stretched as she walked, her joints popping like an old woman's. Getting older was the pits. For a brief moment, she wondered what it would be like to be young and lithe forever—like Riah.

Then again, during some moments when Riah didn't realize anyone watched her, Ivy'd seen pain flash in her eyes. Though Riah never said a word, Ivy had the sense she paid a very high price for her youth and immortality. Still, as Ivy tried to work out the kinks, it was hard not to wish she was twenty again.

The shower worked wonders and, while she didn't feel twenty, it soothed her aching muscles. She'd feel bad about all the aches and pains except getting them was such exquisite pleasure. Colin was a surprise in so many ways, not the least of which was his lovemaking.

Ivy didn't know how to feel about Colin. Falling fast for the guy was scary. People who knew her well would think she'd lost her mind. Falling in love wasn't exactly her strong suit, Jorge being a case in point. So, to find herself in love with a man she barely knew was nuts. And, probably one-sided. No promises had been made. No whispered endearments. He'd simply made love to her, then left her sleeping to go out into the night and slay dragons.

Fairy tales were great, and the good knight on his white horse a wonderful dream. It wasn't the real world. He might very well be a knight on a big white horse, but as soon as this Destiny was six feet under, he'd be gone from her life as quickly as he'd appeared.

Dressed in yesterday's clothes, Ivy sighed and wished she'd brought a clean set. It'd be a lie to say Colin hadn't been on her mind when she'd left Moses Lake, which explained the sexy underwear. Despite slipping into her nicest undies, she'd decided to forego packing an overnight bag. While the underwear seemed hopeful, an overnight bag seemed slutty.

Ivy glanced at the clock and wondered when he'd left. After a vigorous afternoon *workout*, Ivy had ended up falling asleep in his arms. It was easy because he made her feel not only gloriously satisfied, but safe. Held tight in his arms, she'd drifted into blissful rest.

Now, it was very different. The day was wasting and she couldn't lie around waiting for him to return. She made a pot of coffee in the little machine on the desk and waited for it to brew. The whoosh of the water pouring into the carafe was the only sound in the room. She stood gazing out the window as the sun dropped over the mountains to the west. The sky was a brilliant shade of red, and in the distance the lighted towers of the Our Lady of Lourdes Cathedral glowed.

The church made her think of Jorge again. It was hard not to picture him on the cold steel autopsy table. She pushed the bitter memory away. She wanted to remember him as he'd been at her house—handsome, hopeful, and cocky. She said a quick prayer for him and crossed herself.

Ivy drank a cup of the horrible coffee before she grabbed her keys and left the room. A few minutes later, she was driving west. She'd made the trip so many times lately, she felt as though the car could negotiate the route without any help from her. Even the guard at the security gate only nodded when she stopped, then buzzed the gate open.

Riah's car was already in its usual parking space. She expected that. Colin's car was neither inside the gate nor parked on the street. She didn't expect that. That he wasn't already here didn't leave her with a warm and fuzzy feeling. It was bad enough that Colin was absent. The look on Riah's face made her stomach drop even farther. *Shit.*

"What's wrong?" Ivy asked, though terrified of the answer. If something happened to Colin…

Riah shook her head and sighed. "I don't know. Things aren't quite right. The security manager left me a voice mail that one of the guards, a real dedicated guy named A.J., was absent at shift change. Things were locked up and nothing appeared out of the ordinary other than A.J.'s disappearance."

Relief washed over her, though the feeling only lasted a second. A missing guard wasn't a good thing under any circumstances. Given all that had happened lately, her stomach churned. "Have they been able to track him down?"

"No. I talked with the supervisor five minutes ago and, so far, nothing. He's not at his house and he's not answering his cell."

"Maybe he just bailed?" Ivy didn't really believe it even as the words passed her lips.

Riah ran a hand over her eyes. "He's not that kind of guy. I'm usually a pretty good judge of people, Ivy, and I had this guy pegged as one of the good ones."

A bad feeling settled in the pit of her stomach. Nothing was quite as it should be, from the MIA security guard to Riah's strange outfit. Ivy swept her gaze over her friend. Truthfully, she looked somewhere between a dominatrix and a biker bitch. A rather dangerous biker bitch, no less. During all their years as both friends and colleagues, Riah was always classy, but decidedly professional. Tonight, she looked downright menacing.

"Ah, what's with the leather?" Ivy asked.

Riah stared at her for a moment as if the question didn't make sense. Then her eyes cleared. "Battle gear."

"And you're expecting a war?"

"Yes."

Ivy waited. There had to be more than just a simple yes. What kind of war? From whom? Against whom? She understood trouble was on its way, but the details seemed to have whizzed right by her and she was the only one who missed them.

Instead of an explanation, Riah said, "It might be better if you went back home."

"Excuse me?" After everything they'd been through, Riah wanted to shut her out now?

"Seriously, Ivy, there's no need for you to get mixed up in this any more than you already are. Things are going to get bloody, and I'd feel terrible if you got caught in the crosshairs."

Oh, right. For years, they'd worked side-by-side, saving the world from the creatures of darkness, staking vampires, covering up, all the while searching for a cure that might release Riah from the curse. It was just dandy for Ivy to come along for that much of the ride, but now—when things were coming down to the wire—

Riah wanted to send Ivy home like a misbehaving teenager. She had two words for Riah…bull and shit.

"I don't think so." Her words were biting though she managed to keep them civil. It wouldn't do to lose her temper.

"You don't know what you're up against." Riah's dark eyes mirrored the concern in her voice.

Ivy shook her head. Regard for her safety aside, it wasn't fair. She'd earned the right to be here. "Don't know? Are you fucking kidding me?"

Riah said in a quiet voice, "I'm serious."

Ivy waved her hand as if to bat away Riah's words. "Yeah, chica, so am I. I've spent the last ten years as your sidekick, taking heads and writing reports to cover it. I just put my ex-husband down like a rabid dog and fell in love with a guy who hunts vampires, and you have the nerve to stand there and tell me to go home because things are too dangerous!"

"Yes."

The single word uttered in a near-whisper was her undoing. "Screw you, Riah."

Ivy was wound up and ready to get into it. She'd have done it, too, except Adriana sailed in like a flash of lightning headed for Riah.

"Oh, you gorgeous woman." She wrapped Riah in a hug and kissed her.

Riah stepped back, a puzzled look on her face. "What was that for?"

"Oh, like you don't know." Adriana's smile glowed.

Adriana's mood wasn't contagious. There wasn't so much as a trace of a smile on Riah's face. "No, I don't."

Against the dark skin of Adriana's throat, gold glowed and a colored stone flashed. "Is that new?" Ivy asked.

Adriana nodded and held it out. "A gift from my beautiful lover, who's playing innocent." She nudged Riah with a shoulder. Her smile still lit up her face, and no amount of glowering on Riah's part seemed to be able to dampen her joy.

Ivy's gaze shifted from the necklace to Riah's face. What she saw there wasn't what she expected. A look of horror replaced her recent confusion. For a woman who was already pretty damned white, Riah paled even further. What was going on? No one was acting normal and everything seemed…well, wrong.

It seemed to take a huge amount of effort for Riah to get a single question past her lips. Her voice cracked as she asked, "Where did you get that?"

CHAPTER SEVENTEEN

Destiny waited until the attractive black woman drove away before she went to the back of the house. She didn't bother with subtlety. Instead, she shattered the back door with a kick. There was something very satisfying about the sound of breaking glass. Stepping over the splinters and glass shards, Destiny looked around as she walked through the house. An unremarkable kitchen, a very colorful living room, a couple of bedrooms, and a roomy bathroom.

She was missing something. Ah, yes, the basement. She still liked to think of rooms belowground as dungeons, but that was just her. The modern folks liked their basements and didn't appreciate the comparison to dungeons.

Destiny went back to the kitchen and quickly scanned the room. A door against the far wall opened to a staircase leading down. Pay dirt. The room was large and open, and served as the well-stocked working laboratory she'd glimpsed earlier. Gleaming machinery, glass tubes, stainless racks, computers, and whiteboards made a nice facility. This home operation was well-appointed, and Destiny didn't have to be told who the benefactor was.

"Nice try, Catherine," she said as she walked through the room, tipping over bottles and tubes. She yanked cords from the wall and toppled the computers to the floor. No carpet here to soften the impact or save the precious equipment. Good old seasoned concrete made her one-woman party a huge success. The explosion of broken glass, shattering plastic, and draining liquids delighted her.

The mess was fantastic. The room changed from sterile order to odorous chaos. It gave her a nearly orgasmic rush. How she'd love to go through the entire house and blow off steam. Alas, time was a luxury she didn't possess at the moment.

Back outside, Destiny grabbed the can of gasoline she'd earlier stashed in the shrubs. It took less than ten minutes to liberally pour the gasoline throughout the house. The fumes made her eyes water but didn't slow her down.

Once the can was empty, Destiny dropped it to the kitchen floor and made her way outside again, careful not to step in any of the gas. From the back porch, she peered at her handiwork. Her father would be so proud. He liked to tell her being rich was no excuse for being sloppy. Any job was worth doing right.

"Bye-bye," she whispered as she struck a match and tossed it through the frame of the broken door. Flames burst five feet high before spreading like a golden wave as far as she could see. It was a shame she couldn't linger to enjoy her handiwork.

With one deep inhalation, she backed away and smiled wider as she faded into the shadows. She was driving toward the city when the boom of an explosion shattered the quiet night air. A huge burst of light flashed in the rearview mirror.

❖

The blood in Riah's veins turned to ice. It all came to her in a flash and everything fell into place. The insight shook her so deeply, her knees almost buckled.

"Take it off," she rasped.

Adriana tilted her head and peered at Riah as if she'd lost her mind. Her smile faltered for the first time since she'd entered the room. "I don't understand."

Riah's laugh held no humor. "You weren't supposed to understand. You were supposed to put it on and parade it in front of me."

She knew they were all looking at her like she'd gone mad. She didn't blame them. They'd never seen her in full battle mode.

They'd never seen her lose it so badly her voice shook and her body trembled.

The Riah they knew was a calm, rational, and conservative doctor, and very real to Ivy and Adriana. Even to Colin for the brief amount of time they'd known each other. In reality, Riah Preston didn't exist. Riah was the personification of everything she wanted to be: the doctor, the researcher, the saver of lives. She was good and kind, and in love.

She was also a big, fat liar.

Adriana studied Riah's face. Something must have clicked because she undid the clasp and slipped the gorgeous piece into Riah's outstretched hand. Riah closed her fingers over the stone.

She dropped into a chair and stared at the necklace glittering in her palm. The hardness of the precious metal and the coolness of the stone took her into the past and she had to blink back tears.

"I owe you all an explanation," she said when she could talk without her voice breaking.

Ivy put a hand on her shoulder. "Riah, you don't owe us anything. Besides, whatever it is, we'll understand."

Her stomach rolled as she took a deep breath. "I doubt it."

Both Adriana and Ivy were incredible women. They were smart, dedicated, and understanding. What she was about to tell them would stretch even the most understanding of people. She'd tell them the whole ugly truth. It was time to stop hiding.

"Don't sell us short," Adriana said as she knelt next to Riah and took one of her hands. "We're all in this together."

For the first time in many, many years, tears formed in Riah's eyes. She took a deep breath and plunged forward. "My name isn't Riah Preston."

❖

At the base of the steps, Colin paused. Time was running out and it wasn't a good idea to spend any of it here. Yet he didn't seem able to walk away. He ran a hand through his hair, then started to climb past the statues and toward the huge carved doors. Our Lady of Lourdes was carved into the granite over the entrance.

He could use the Lady's wisdom tonight. If little Bernadette Soubiroux could go searching for firewood and encounter the Blessed Virgin Mary back in 1858, why couldn't he when searching for enlightenment?

In the far back and close to the exit, he slid into a pew. For a minute he simply sat there with his hands folded. Though he felt peaceful, nothing else filled him.

Colin sighed and lowered the kneeling board. On his knees, he rested his head on his hands. "Give me something, God," he whispered. "Show me the way."

Footsteps fell lightly in the quiet. Colin raised his head. A priest walked his way, tall and smiling, his sandy hair cut short and close to his head. The man wasn't much older than Colin.

"Welcome." He extended his hand. "I'm Father Jason. Is there something I can help you with?"

Colin shook the offered hand. "I don't think so, but thank you."

Father Jason studied him closely, and the scrutiny made Colin want to squirm.

"You're a hunter," Father Jason said as he sat in the pew next to Colin.

The surprise brought Colin up from the kneeling board. "Excuse me?"

"A hunter," he said patiently, as if talking to a small child.

"You know?" Colin sank slowly to the pew again.

His blue eyes were earnest. "I could lie and say I'm all-knowing, except I'm not. I'm a simple parish priest. The truth is, Monsignor called me earlier and told me to expect you."

"How?"

"I said I'm not all-knowing. I didn't say Monsignor wasn't."

Colin leaned back and shook his head. "Impossible." Yet it wasn't. Monsignor possessed the most uncanny ability to understand what people needed even before they knew it themselves. He'd been proving that to Colin for a great many years. Today was no exception.

Father Jason laid a hand on Colin's arm. "He said you're having a crisis of faith."

Colin shook his head slowly. "Not exactly. Faith isn't the problem right now."

"No?"

"No. It's everything else."

"I have time," Father Jason told him.

"Unfortunately, I don't."

Colin stood and started to move out of the pew. It might be nice to talk to the man, but he was tempting fate as it was by stopping. Destiny was out there, and until she was taken down, no one was safe. He had to go. His personal struggles would have to wait for another day.

Father Jason's voice followed him as he walked back toward the doors. "Recall the words of Psalms 85:10-11. Mercy and truth are met together; righteousness and peace have kissed each other. Truth shall spring out of the earth; and righteousness shall look down from heaven."

At the door Colin stopped and looked back to the priest who stood at the end of the pew, his hands folded. It was as if the man could read his mind. He met the priest's eyes, nodded, and left.

All the way to the morgue, those words rang in his mind. If only things could be easy. He'd been in numerous battles and not one had filled him with such chaos. Tonight, it was all about taking Destiny down. If he concentrated on that one goal, everything else would work out…he hoped.

The gate was unattended when he arrived at the PSB, and any other time he would find it suspicious. Nothing was ordinary at the moment, not even security. He drove through and parked his car.

Inside he followed the low murmur of voices and slowly pushed open the doors to the autopsy suite. Riah, Adriana, and Ivy stood talking. He glanced briefly at Riah and Adriana, his gaze coming to rest on Ivy. She didn't look at him.

He forced his attention away from Ivy to concentrate on what Riah was saying and was shocked. The last thing he expected to hear coming from her mouth was the truth.

Colin stepped farther into the room until he propped himself against a cabinet with his arms crossed over his chest. "Catherine Tudor," he said, his deep voice echoing in the large room.

❖

At the sound of Colin's voice, Riah snapped her head up. "How did you know?" She honestly believed the truth of her true identity had died hundreds of years ago.

"I wasn't sure. Not until this morning."

"Your superiors with their archives and their vault full of secrets?" Even though she believed her identity was lost to the ages, at the same time she didn't underestimate the resources of his church.

It was Colin's turn to nod. "We've known for a good many years of your existence, we just couldn't find you. You've done a very good job of hiding in plain sight."

"It's been my dirty secret for nearly five hundred years and, frankly, I'm tired of it. My whole life, both as a mortal and as a vampire, has been nothing but lies. I don't want to lie or hide any longer."

Adriana stroked Riah's head. "I don't believe that. Maybe your name is a lie, but your heart isn't. I've never met anyone as honest as you."

Riah wiped tears away with the back of her hand. "Just another deception, Adriana. Sad but true. It started from the moment I was born. My father, my birth father—King Henry VII—didn't want me. The queen was gravely ill and there I was, a puny little girl. I was exactly what he didn't want, especially if the queen was to die. If I'd been a boy, things would have been much different."

"I'm no history genius," Ivy said, her forehead creased in concentration. "But I don't remember Henry VIII having a baby sister."

Riah nodded and crossed her arms over her chest. "That's because I supposedly died at birth. If you go back into the history records, my father sent a message to his people about the sad passing of his infant daughter. It was all very formal and very much false."

"So how…" Adriana tilted her head and studied Riah.

"Father used me as ante in a card game. A fine Lord, one of my father's trusted confidants, won the hand and a baby girl. His Lady desired a child and couldn't have one of her own, so voila, I was bundled up and smuggled out of the castle to be raised as the daughter of the Lord and Lady."

"That's fucked up," Adriana said as she stroked Riah's arm.

Riah barely felt the touch of her lover's hand as she began to speak slowly. "It was all fine until I turned seventeen and Mother died. Once she was gone, my adoptive father was less than interested in his *daughter.* He'd cared enough for his wife to provide her with a child, but he cared nothing for me. He'd keep up appearances only because of his agreement with King Henry. If not for what happened the night Rodolphe turned me, I'd have been married off to some old geezer and out of his hair for good. Either way, it worked out for Father because I was gone. My so-called death didn't send him into mourning."

"What happened?" Colin's question was soft, without the hard edge she expected.

She closed her eyes and took a deep breath. Honestly, she didn't want to remember. For five centuries, she'd embraced a self-imposed amnesia, though the ploy didn't work well and too often the memories assaulted her anyway. Not once had she ever told another living soul what happened to her or to Meriel.

Times change. People change, and it was past time for her to change. She began to talk. "Meriel, that is Lady Meriel Danson, my best friend…my lover, and I were in the back of the carriage. We were on our way home from a ball held at the country home of Lord Clifford Savard. It had been a glorious party, and both Meriel and I were very popular. You must understand, we were at the most desirable age and at the height of our beauty. I remember dancing and laughing, and leaving the party happy. We'd made love in the carriage and then I fell asleep. I awoke when the driver brought the horses to a stop, and after that everything happened in a blur."

"You were attacked." Colin wasn't asking a question this time.

Riah nodded. "Rodolphe." His name tasted bitter on her tongue.

"I know of him," Colin said thoughtfully. "Destroyed sometime around the time of the American Revolution. Not a nice man either before or after he was turned. Cut quite a bloody path through Europe."

"Your records are accurate," she told him. "Rodolphe was a cruel man in life and merciless in undeath. But he was beautiful and persuasive. He made you want to be with him. I was just as susceptible to his charms as any other woman or vampire, and I wasn't into men, if you get my drift. Do they mention me at his side?" Riah asked quietly.

Adriana gasped and her hand tightened on Riah's arm. "No."

"Yes," Colin said.

"I'd be surprised if I wasn't part of your records on Rodolphe," she said to Colin, though she looked up to meet Adriana's startled gaze. It was difficult to look into Adriana's eyes and bare her soul. It was equally difficult not to. Adriana deserved to know the truth, even as ugly as it was. The woman Adriana professed to love didn't really exist, and it was only fair to give her the straight facts.

Riah covered Adriana's hand with hers. "I was everything the legends make a vampire out to be. Bloodthirsty, cruel, and relentless. I was the monster my brother intended me to become and Rodolphe molded me into."

"Your brother?" Colin blinked, a shocked expression on his face.

She raised an eyebrow. It didn't surprise her to know they'd managed to uncover everything about her history, including her blood relationship to Henry VIII. Despite her biological father's attempt to keep the truth of her parentage a secret, even back then, rumors persisted long after his death. It would have surprised her a great deal if they knew of the connection her brother had with Rodolphe. She very much doubted anyone still alive knew how her brother was involved with her transition from life to undeath.

"Your research missed that little tidbit, didn't it?" she asked.

Colin gave her a curt nod, a slight frown on his lips. "I'd have to say yes, since I'm really not sure what you're telling us. What did Henry have to do with you and Rodolphe?"

Riah explained. "My older brother, who sat on the throne after the death of our father in 1509, discovered the whole dirty secret of my birth not long before my fateful carriage ride. Let it suffice to say, he wasn't pleased. Not only did he not want yet another sister, he also didn't want to have to deal with the ramifications if the unsavory secret of my birth was known. I think big brother was quite worried my adoptive father intended to send me back to the royal family if he couldn't secure a proper husband for me. Brother dear wasn't about to allow that to happen. Henry, I was to find out much later, possessed secrets of his own, including a friend who just happened to be a handsome vampire."

"Rodolphe?" Ivy asked.

Riah continued, keeping her voice calm. "I was set up, and Meriel, the true innocent in all of it, was caught in the crossfire. It didn't quite go down like Henry planned either. I was the one who was supposed to die, not Meriel. Rodolphe's agreement with Henry was to kill me and keep Meriel as his prize. Of course, I only learned of these things much later. The night I was turned, I still had no idea I was the daughter of a dead king and sister to the reigning king. Shortly afterward, I discovered the truth of my birth and that I was, in fact, a princess. Even then, it was a long time until I learned all of the truth. Until Rodolphe shared the details of his deal with my brother, I believed I was simply in the wrong place at the wrong time."

"Oh, Riah, how terrible for you." Adriana put her arms around Riah and hugged her tight.

The comfort Adriana offered was irrelevant at the moment. Her emotions were still wrapped around the betrayals so prevalent in her life. Riah didn't really like to think about those days. Not about what she lost, not about what she learned about her real identity, and certainly not about what she ultimately became. She blamed Henry for setting it all into motion, even if she couldn't blame him for all she became afterward.

She could fault Rodolphe for leading her down the awful path if it weren't for the fact she went willingly. Even more, she'd followed him joyfully. At least in the early years. The discovery of immortality and the power it provided was beyond exhilarating. The feelings it invoked were indescribable.

Rodolphe didn't force her to embrace the darkness; he simply encouraged her. It was freedom like she'd never experienced before. Certainly there were limitations and she learned to be very careful. Still, it was so much more than her role as a young, rich woman ever could have given her. Intoxicating. She took his gift of darkness and didn't look back for a very long time.

Riah made her own choices back then, and she had to live with the consequences of her actions even now. She had little to be proud of in those days. All she was left with once she moved beyond the dark life was the will to make amends. She wanted to set her karmic scale back into balance.

But, no matter how many years passed or how far she ran, Riah couldn't escape her past. The scales would always be tipped, and not in her favor. The truth stood in front of her now in the form of a vampire hunter.

From the very first day of her rebirth, shadows hovered on her trail just beyond her line of sight. She could never quite make them out, but she always knew they were there and would one day catch up.

"I don't deserve your pity," she told Adriana as she gazed into her eyes. "I was a monster and now it's time to pay for all the grief and heartache I caused so many innocent people."

Adriana's fingers stroked her cheek, her touch warm against Riah's cool flesh. Her heart fluttered in a way it hadn't in five hundred years, and tears welled in her eyes again. She willed them not to fall. If ever there was a time to be strong, it was now. Besides, she didn't deserve pity…not even her own.

Except it wasn't fair and, for once, she didn't feel like being strong. She never thought she'd be able to love another woman, yet out of the blue, it'd happened again. The bitter truth was Riah loved Adriana with all her heart, and now she'd lose once more.

For such a long time now, she'd done her best to do the right thing. It was a gigantic mountain to climb yet, sometimes, she actually felt as though she made progress. Something good came out of the long years of work.

Now, none of it mattered any longer. Outside a storm raged, invisible to all but the chosen few who could see beyond the veil of the natural world and into the preternatural realm. Even in this room, surrounded by people who could understand, it was difficult to find the words to warn them. What would become of her didn't matter any longer. Her die had been cast long ago. These people, however, mattered—even the hunter.

Before she could say anything else, the door swung slowly open. Though the hinges were oiled, the swish of the doors sweeping across the tiled floor made them all turn. There were a fair number of people she'd expect to walk through the doors this time of night, but the one who did came as a complete surprise.

Riah forgot all about her own guilt and self-pity. The storm had just arrived and, in response, she muttered two words. "Oh, shit."

CHAPTER EIGHTEEN

Ivy recognized the man who stepped through the open door even though he was white as paste and moving with awkward, shuffling steps like he was old and very ill. He was neither. The young security guard who'd walked her to her car a couple of times pushed open the door and headed for Riah.

The last time Ivy saw the guy, he was tall and vibrant with tanned skin and intelligent eyes. Though he was a fair bit younger than Ivy, she'd thought he was kinda hot. Little of his previous appearance remained as he slid dirty boots across the floor, leaving dark streaks on the tile as he moved. His gaze never wavered from Riah's face, his eyes dark and empty. Ivy had the feeling he was unaware that others were even in the room. His expression gave her the creeps.

Colin was the first to shake off the shock. While the rest of them stood motionless and staring, he moved like wildfire. Ivy was surprised by his quick, agile movements. Sure, he was dynamic in bed, but he was naked in bed and not hampered by clothes, boots, and a long jacket. Fully dressed, he still moved with the impressive fluidity and speed of the native mountain lions that roamed the hills around Spokane.

From beneath his coat, Colin drew a sword. *"Hijo de puta,"* Ivy murmured.

Swear to God, the man just pulled from inside the folds of his leather coat a full-out gleaming length of steel with razor edges and a fancy hilt. Ivy couldn't figure out where he'd had the thing hidden. Even more perplexing was why she didn't notice it before. Sure, his coat was long and flowing—a look pretty hot, by the way—but wouldn't she have noticed a sword?

He held the lethal-looking weapon high, gripped with both hands, his legs parted, and his eyes focused on the young man's ghostly face. A warrior's stance, and it struck her suddenly that this was a war. Not the *normal* kind of conflict learned about in history class. Quite the contrary, this was a battle with no rules and no clear-cut idea of exactly who the enemy was. All wars sucked, but this one sucked even worse.

Riah sprang from the chair. Similar to Colin, she moved like a cat, silently and predatory. From beneath the folds of her black leather coat, she also pulled a gleaming sword. *"¿Qué diablos?"* Ivy exclaimed.

Was she the only one who didn't have medieval weapons stuffed in her outerwear? She cut a glance Adriana's way, relieved to see she wasn't pulling weapons out of her clothes. The most lethal thing Ivy had on her person at the moment was a set of car keys. Nothing like showing up at a sword fight with…well, nothing.

Before she could worry about her lack of weaponry, she shifted her attention back to Riah, who moved so quickly, she was a blur even in the brightly lit room. In a flash, Riah stood before the pasty-faced man whose name tag read Andrew. What she saw was less than reassuring. In the years since Riah's secret had been revealed to her, she'd watched as Riah took the heads of vampire victims in order to spare them from an existence of not-quite-life and not-quite-death. In each case, those victims had been flat on their backs and, more often than not, on a stainless-steel table just like the one in front of her now. She'd never seen one rise.

Until now.

"Who made you?" Riah demanded of the security guard in the wrinkled, filthy uniform.

By the look of him, she'd have said he'd spent an entire week sleeping in his clothes. She knew better. Twenty-four hours ago, this same guard stood in the door of the facility, watching her get into her car. His clothes had been clean, his eyes alive, and his soul intact.

Tonight, he smiled and Ivy shivered at the sight of his pointed canines, glistening damply red. His eyes were empty, as if the person he once was no longer existed inside his youthful body.

"You know," he murmured. "Our friend."

"I've no friends like that," she spat back.

Riah's battle stance never changed and her eyes were hard.

"I think you're wrong." Andrew laughed.

The sound was brittle and ugly. It sent goose bumps racing up Ivy's arms and she took a step back. Another step and she was behind Colin, who still stood on alert with his sword at the ready. It made her feel just a little safer to be behind his strong back while he held a sharp weapon in strike position. She stuck her hand in her pocket, curling her fingers around the car keys.

"Who?" Riah's voice rose to a near-scream and the sword in her hands trembled. Ivy wasn't sure if it was from fury or fright.

"Meriel." Andrew drew the name out in a long, wistful breath. Then he licked his lips and his dead eyes narrowed. They were black slits in his pasty-white face. A thin thread of red dripped from the corner of his mouth.

The name hung in the air only seconds before Riah's sword flashed. Everything seemed to happen in slow motion as the dark head tumbled through the air before falling to the floor with a wet thump.

Stifling a gasp, Ivy turned away. The sight of the young man's head turning over and over through the air was something she wished she could erase from her vision. His eyes were open, a hint of a smile curving around the bloody fangs. Drops of crimson blood sprayed everywhere, landing on the walls, the floor, and the stainless-steel table. Colin lowered his sword to his side and used his free arm to pull Ivy close to him. He felt strong and real while everything around her seemed dreamlike.

He kissed the top of her head. "Maybe it would be better if you left," he said gently against her hair.

She trembled, though his words made her straighten up. For a moment she was tempted to flee. It'd be easy to run and hide, to pretend none of this was real. Except it was, and even if she ran away, it wouldn't change a thing. Vampires would still exist and one of them had killed Jorge.

Ivy looked into Colin's face and was warmed by what she saw in his eyes. It gave her strength. "No," she said as she squeezed his hand. "I'm staying."

"He's probably right," Riah added. "In fact, I think both you and Adriana should get out of here now."

She turned her gaze from Colin's face to Riah's. "We can help you."

It was important to stay and to help. It was more than simply avenging Jorge's death. Among other things, Ivy didn't want to leave Colin. If she did, she might never see him again.

Riah's gaze was hard as she met Ivy's eyes. This woman she'd never seen before both scared her and made her more determined not to leave.

"Colin was right before. A.J. is just the first. There'll be more and they'll be more powerful and more dangerous," Riah said.

Colin had tossed out to them earlier the idea that Destiny had crossed the country creating an army as she went. He didn't know why, only that the number of victims found didn't equal the number of those missing. The simple math pointed to the potential of a cadre of young vampires. Earlier when Colin floated his theory, Ivy thought it was out there. Way out there. Now—not so much.

Of course, if he was right, and an army was on its way, it didn't make sense for either her or Adriana to leave. Once again, simple math meant four fighters were bound to be more useful than only two, even if those two were very, very experienced. Oh, and don't forget, one of the two just happened to be a vampire. Still, it didn't change the numbers, and in Ivy's mind, right now, numbers ruled. Mathematics always won the day.

"I'm not leaving." Ivy tightened her grip on Colin's arm. Beneath his coat, she could feel the slightest tremor. Fear or adrenaline?

He shook his head. "It's not safe for you or Adriana. You've no idea what you're up against."

She raised an eyebrow and pointed at the bloody remains of the security guard. "Wrong there, Sherlock…I've got more than a clue." Colin sighed and shook his head again. "Damn it, Ivy. This is nothing. Nothing!"

"He's right," Riah chimed in. "A.J. wasn't a threat. He was a warning. What's coming for us is old and dangerous, and backed up by young, hungry vampires. You've no idea how vicious the young can be. They have only one thing on their mind: blood. They'll tear you apart. If I've seen it once, I've seen it a hundred times, and it isn't pretty."

She understood Riah and Colin's scare tactics. If she was in their shoes, she'd do the same thing. It changed nothing.

"I'm not leaving." Ivy looked over at Adriana, who nodded. She saw her own resolve mirrored in Adriana's face. "*We're* not leaving," she added, and dug her fingers into Colin's arm.

"Oh, for Christ's sake." Riah exploded. She whirled to glare at Adriana. "Don't you get it? I know you're not stupid but what you're doing is. If you stay here, you'll die. I can't protect you."

"I'm not leaving," Adriana whispered, not backing away in the face of Riah's angry outburst. "I can't."

"Neither am I," Ivy said.

Before anyone else could protest, an explosion made them all stop. At the same time, the walls shook and the doors rattled.

"What the—" Riah turned and raced to the desk tucked into a corner of the big room. She clicked furiously at the keys on her computer. The emergency-call system came alive with the sound of frantic voices.

It didn't mean much to Ivy. An explosion on Northwest Boulevard had emergency personnel on the run. The preliminary report said that a home in the quiet residential area was completely destroyed.

"Oh, my God," Adriana cried, and clapped her hands to her mouth.

Riah pulled Adriana into her arms and looked over her head at Ivy and Colin. "It's Adriana's house," she explained.

"Not good," Colin said, a dark look on his face. "I don't like coincidences."

"Oh my God, oh my God," Adriana muttered into Riah's shoulder, her entire body shaking.

"It'll be all right," Riah murmured into her hair.

Adriana pulled away. "You don't understand. This isn't just terrible. This is catastrophic."

"You can stay with me," Riah told her.

"It's not that." Adriana's voice rose.

"Tell us," Ivy urged softly, hoping to calm the panic rising in Adriana. The look on her face made Ivy nervous. Whatever this was, it wasn't about having a place to live.

Tears began to stream down Adriana's face. "I succeeded. I found the cure."

Riah's sword clattered to the floor and she took a step away from Adriana, appearing totally shocked. "You did it?"

Adriana nodded. "That's what I really came down to tell you tonight. I found the cure. I could've made you human again."

"Could have?" Ivy asked. She didn't miss the past tense even if it seemed to fly right on by Riah.

Adriana's tears came harder. "Everything was at my home. All my notes, all my research, everything. I even thought I was so smart because I backed everything up on a flash drive."

"You left the flash drive at home," Ivy said.

Adriana nodded and began to cry even harder. Ivy wanted to cry right along with her.

"And it just blew sky-high." Colin stated the obvious.

Her children were waiting just as she'd instructed them to. They were an obedient bunch. Destiny did so love the young. They were excited and awed by the new dimension to their existence. Everything she showed them was intriguing. They were quick to learn, loved to kill, and were always up for a challenge. Not just for the food either. Whatever the reason, killing appealed to young vampires.

Oh, yes, there was the occasional odd-ball, the vampire who took exception to the nature of his or her changed existence. They were the ones who couldn't reconcile their immortality with the necessity of blood to survive. They either died quickly or became outcasts in the vampire society, living in the shadows and surviving off the blood of animals. These lesser vampires, in Destiny's opinion, were a waste of time and energy. Well, except for one. One of these oddities held a very special place in Destiny's heart.

"Is everyone here?" Destiny directed her question to a lovely young woman of about nineteen with long red hair and sky blue eyes. Bella was one of her oldest children and far from the ragged girl she'd turned in a filthy London alley.

Stinking and near-starvation, Bella at first seemed nothing more than a meal. But beneath the dirt and stench, Destiny glimpsed something special. She hadn't been wrong.

"All but the newest of our flock," Bella answered.

Destiny wasn't surprised. Bella wasn't only beautiful, she was efficient. "He returned to the morgue?"

Bella nodded. "Just as you wished."

"Perfect."

Five sets of eyes watched her, waiting. Outside the upscale restaurant, they captured little attention as they stood in a cluster on the sidewalk. Just a small group of friends out for a night on the town, because they were well-dressed and beautiful, their unusually pale skin, the dark eyes, or the elongated canines weren't readily apparent.

"Shall we attack?" Bella asked, licking her lips. Her eyes sparkled in the darkness, and the others, seeming to anticipate a bloody battle, gathered close.

Destiny laid a hand on Bella's arm. "Easy, my love."

"But I'm hungry," whined Ford, a tall, muscled twenty-something hottie she'd found in the flatlands of Nebraska.

Beautiful as he was, Ford was also very young and difficult to control. He possessed a voracious hunger for both blood and sex. Anytime, anywhere, with anyone. He loved women and men. One at a time was fine, or two, or three. Destiny had Bella keep a really close eye on him so he didn't get into trouble.

Destiny kissed Ford on the lips. "Patience, my prince. You'll have plenty to feast on soon." She pressed her hand into his crotch, smiling at the instant hard-on. "I promise."

Ford smiled and pushed his hips into her hand. "After it's done?"

"I'll fuck your brains out."

"Deal."

"Me too," chimed in Emily.

In a low-cut top and tight jeans, Emily should look like a tramp except she didn't. She was a rare beauty who looked barely old enough to drive but had, in fact, been thirty-two years old when Destiny turned her.

Destiny ran a hand over Emily's breasts, smiling as her nipples sprang up hard. "The more the merrier."

The twins didn't say anything but they didn't have to. The invitation was issued and accepted. Always quiet, Mara and Markus listened, learned, and became hunters of the first order. In any battle, the twins were a definite asset. In bed, they were even better.

Overhead, the moon glowed bright in the clear night sky. When she'd left the black woman's house, the moon had been just cresting the mountains. Now, it was directly overhead. Perfect.

"Come, my loves, it's time to get this party started."

CHAPTER NINETEEN

R iah sank once more into a chair, her boots hitting her sword where it lay on the floor. God, she was tired. What was the point of any of this? It didn't matter what she did or how she tried to make things better, it ultimately all blew up.

Adriana knelt beside her and took Riah's face in her hands. "Don't," Adriana said softly.

Riah met her gaze and frowned. "It doesn't make any difference."

"It makes a difference to me. I love you, Riah."

Didn't she see? "I'm not Riah. I wanted to be. I wanted to be something besides the unwanted child of a King, the unwanted sister of a King, or the sidekick of a master vampire. I wanted to try to make things right and be human again. Instead, I've managed to put you all in danger and destroy the one thing that could have helped."

"It's not your fault," Adriana said.

"It's all my fault. None of you would be here if not for me."

Adriana stroked her cheek. "Well, I can't speak for Ivy or Colin but I gotta tell ya, Doc, that while things might be a little screwed up right at the moment, my life has been more exciting since I met you than ever before. I can't imagine not having you in it."

Riah closed her eyes and sighed as she rested her cheek in Adriana's hand. She'd love to believe Adriana and to allow herself the comfort she offered. She didn't dare let her guard down or put any of these people into more danger.

Slowly, she stood and took a step away from Adriana. "Thank you, Adriana. I think now, however, it would be a good idea if you all left."

Ivy was the first to speak. "What?"

"Seriously," Riah said. "You three should get out of here before the shit hits the fan."

"Not a chance," Colin said in a low, quiet voice.

"Look," Riah countered. "I know you're experienced and all, but this is my fight. I don't see any reason for you to stay. Unless…"

Colin's eyes held hers. No need to finish the thought. He was on the same wavelength. She'd give him credit, he was sharp.

"Unless what?" Ivy demanded.

Riah's gaze never wavered from the man's face. "Do you want to tell her or shall I?"

"Somebody better spill it." Ivy gave Riah a quick glance before turning her gaze on Colin.

Colin winced when Ivy stared at him, her dark eyes full of sparks. He didn't speak. Riah had the impression he was afraid to.

Adriana's voice was soft. "I think Riah doesn't see any reason for Colin to stay unless he plans on taking her head."

"She's a vampire," Ivy whispered.

Colin nodded.

Ivy grabbed him with both hands. "You can't."

Riah felt bad for her friend. Ivy didn't really get it even though she'd been at Riah's side for years. "It's what he does, Ivy."

"Colin." Ivy pleaded. "Tell me you won't kill her."

"She's already dead," he murmured, his eyes on Ivy's face.

"He's right, you know," Riah said. "I've been the walking dead for five centuries. He'll just be putting me out of my misery."

"No!"

All three of them turned to look at Adriana. Her hands were on her hips and her eyes blazed. She was breathing hard.

"Enough from all you. Pull your heads out of your asses. We're on the same goddamn team. Do you get it? The same fucking team!"

Riah was probably more startled than any of them. She'd never heard Adriana raise her voice. She was one of the calmest, most level-headed people Riah'd ever met.

"We're in this together, boys and girls. Nobody's leaving, nobody's destroying anyone, and we're fighting side by side. Got it?"

Silence hung for a full minute as they stared at Adriana. Then Riah started to laugh.

"This is fucking bizarre," she said when she caught her breath. "But I'm in, if you are."

"Colin?" Ivy asked.

He shook his head and sighed. "The monsignor is going to have my hide."

"Is that a yes?" Ivy touched his cheek.

He took her hand and kissed the palm. His eyes were on Riah's face as he answered. "That's a yes."

Colin wasn't kidding when he said the monsignor would have his hide. He was breaking the absolute rule of a hunter. His mission had one goal: to destroy vampires. *All vampires.* Not only was he about to let one live, he was getting ready to fight beside her. It went against everything in his life.

Of course, things had changed over the last few weeks. He'd felt it before he even saw Ivy. Something in the universe shifted and he was caught in the wave. Then he'd seen Ivy on the shores of Moses Lake and something else gave way.

Whatever he might have to reconcile with later would have to be dealt with later. The immediate problem was somewhere outside that door and required every ounce of his concentration.

The young man whose remains lay bloody on the floor was only the first. Destiny was coming, and she wasn't coming alone. This would be something akin to the fight at the OK Corral. It was the final gun battle except guns wouldn't help. A nice shotgun might slow Destiny and her minions down, but that was all. This would be a bloody battle of wits and swords. The last man standing would be the one who still had his head.

He held Ivy's hand, grateful for the warmth of her flesh. Just the feel of her hand gave him courage. Not the fighting kind. He'd spent his entire adult life battling creatures no one should have to face. He was tough and able to hold his own.

No, the courage she gave him had everything to do with needing to face down the enemy and come out the victor. He always fought to win, but if his life was lost, it would be the price paid for a greater good. Now, for the first time, he had something to fight for. Not just for the world at large, but for him as well. He wanted to live through this battle for Ivy.

"So what do you think, Riah?"

"I think," Riah said slowly, "that for whatever reason, Destiny has been trying to isolate me."

"And I unwittingly helped."

She nodded. "A few nights ago," she said, "I made some calls."

"To other vampires," he added.

Riah nodded. "Vampires I trusted. I couldn't reach a single one. A little bit of research and I uncovered information on their deaths."

He wasn't surprised. "They've all been destroyed just as I told you."

"Yes."

"So, basically, I helped her out." He'd reached the same conclusion earlier.

"Yes."

"And now?" He tightened his hand around Ivy's.

A smile with no humor crossed Riah's face. "Now, she thinks she's gotten her way."

"And now, you're confusing me," Ivy chimed in.

"Stay with me for a few minutes," Riah told them. "Remember how I told you I had a lover back in my first life? When our carriage was attacked, I saw Meriel lying dead on the side of the road. The necklace," she pointed to where it lay on the counter, "was on her throat when Rodolphe carried me away."

"And…" Colin still wasn't quite following.

"And," Riah said slowly, "I think the one who left it at Adriana's house was Meriel."

It finally dawned on him. "Destiny."

Riah inclined her head his way. "Yes."

"Why now?" It seemed to Colin if what Riah said was true, Destiny would have come after her a long time ago. Why wait five centuries?

Riah shrugged. "That's the million-dollar question. I saw her cold and dead on that road. Now, I'm not so sure. I'm thinking Destiny and Meriel are one and the same. I feel it here." She tapped her chest.

"And she's coming here," Adriana whispered.

Riah turned her gaze to Adriana. "Yes."

"She's bringing company too," Colin reminded them. He could feel it in his bones. The sort of buzz that happened every time he stepped into battle.

"She destroyed my house." Adriana wasn't asking a question.

For the first time, the pieces seemed to fall into place for Adriana too. Ivy was pretty quiet, though Colin knew she was on the same page. He could feel the slight tremors in her body as he held her hand. Her face betrayed nothing. She looked determined and ready.

He'd really like for Ivy and Adriana to go somewhere safe. Truth be told, this wasn't Ivy's battle. Sure, Destiny had killed her ex-husband, which made it personal. On the other hand, the man had been a part of her past. She could let this stay in the hands of those more qualified to fight.

This battle was between Riah and the woman she'd left for dead along a dark, wooded road. It was also a battle between him and a vampire because, first and foremost, he was a vampire hunter.

Funny, though, right now he felt less like a vampire hunter and more like a man who wanted to run far away with his woman. Somewhere safe and warm. He wanted to forget about monsters and demons, take her in his arms, and kiss her all over.

His wishes didn't matter. He didn't matter. Destroying an evil being that fed off the lives of innocent people did. Destiny had to be destroyed along with those she'd brought with her. He'd believed his journey was nearly at an end and only two vampires remained.

He'd been wrong. There'd be no running away with the woman he loved. First, he'd have to stand up and pay for his error. It could very well cost him his life.

Colin turned to Ivy. He took both hands in his this time and looked deep into her beautiful dark eyes. "Please go home to Moses Lake," he pleaded. "Please do this for me."

She shook her head. "No."

"You don't understand."

"You don't understand. Jorge lost his life to this bitch, and I'll be damned if I'll run and hide while she tries to take yours. I've loved two men in my life. She's taken one. She's not taking the other. *Comprende?*"

Yes, he understood. He didn't think she did. "I can take care of myself."

She squeezed his hands. "I know, but I'm still not leaving. Crazy as this sounds…crazy as this is, Colin, I think…no, I know… I'm in love with you."

"I understand."

She looked surprised. "You too?"

"Yeah, me too."

"Thank God," she whispered. "It's confusing enough, but it helps you're right here with me."

He pulled her close and kissed the top of her head. "I'm very much with you on that one, sweetheart." He kissed her again. "You're sure you won't wait for me back in Moses Lake?"

"Not a chance."

"Well, then here's how this is gonna go down."

CHAPTER TWENTY

Outside the security fence, Destiny paused. The parking lot was dark. Every other time she'd been here, a security light over the rear entrance to the medical examiner's offices illuminated the lot. Now, it was as black as ink.

She smiled. *Nice try, Catherine. It'll take more than darkness to stop me.*

"Mara, Markus." She waited for the two black-haired beauties to reach her before waving toward the dark parking lot. "Check the yard and clear out any debris."

Mara, her gleaming black hair pulled back with an ornate silver clip, smiled. Her elongated fangs glistened. "Of course, Mistress."

Markus said nothing, which wasn't unusual.

Silently, the two leapt over the fence like a pair of gazelles and blended into the shadows. Destiny and the others waited, although she far more patiently than her restless, hungry, and horny children. She heard a soft thud and, moments later, a second one, and smiled.

When the twins didn't return quickly, Destiny frowned. It wasn't like them not to show up as soon as they cleared a path. She moved to the fence and listened. Nothing. A bad feeling tickled at the back of her neck before the entrance gate began to slide slowly open. She let out a breath and allowed the smile to return.

Destiny motioned for the others to follow her through. Inside the gate, she stopped and inhaled deeply. The air was filled with many scents, including fresh blood. As soon as their work was done, they'd gorge on the spoils of victory.

She waited for the twins to rejoin them. The hair at the back of her neck tingled again. This wasn't like Markus or Mara. Enough. She couldn't afford to get sidetracked. Catherine wasn't a foe to take lightly. Destiny closed her eyes and stilled, concentrating on what the night carried in its embrace. All of a sudden, the scent of blood in the air took on a different quality. So did the silence. The tingle she'd felt a moment earlier turned to something far darker.

Destiny's fury built. "Bella," she roared "Find them."

On full alert, Ford and Emily flanked her.

"Do you want me to go with Bella?" Ford asked in a low voice. His body was tense, his hands in fists at his sides.

It might be a good idea except she feared the situation wasn't as it seemed. Bella was strong and experienced. She could defend herself, if need be.

"No." She laid a hand on Ford's arm, the muscles taut beneath her palm. "We'll wait."

Bella returned in less than a minute, heralded by the faint sound of wet drops hitting the asphalt: plink, plink, plink. Even in the darkness, Destiny made out what Bella held in each hand. The sightless eyes of the twins stared into the night as Bella's fingers gripped their long black hair. Blood dripped from what was left of their necks. The cuts were clean and even.

Until now, this had been more of a game. Certainly Destiny's plans all along included killing her long-ago lover, but that was more for a taste of karma than revenge. Catherine had abandoned her like a rabid dog, leaving her for dead in the mud and darkness. Tonight she intended to return the favor.

Except the game had just changed. Killing her children made everything different. If Catherine wanted to play dirty, then so be it.

Destiny lifted her head and let loose a blood-curdling scream. "I'm coming for you, Catherine Tudor, and I'm bringing all the circles of hell with me."

❖

"The circles of hell?" Adriana looked at Riah with eyebrows raised.

"Dante's 'Inferno,'" she said. "She's letting me know she is, in fact, Meriel." *A mighty flame followeth a tiny spark.* She remembered Dante's words as if Meriel had read them to her just yesterday.

"Why Dante?" Colin asked.

"It was one of our secrets. We were forbidden to study Dante, so we smuggled *The Divine Comedy* into her bedchambers to read. I think we were both ultimately destined for the dark side."

"Dante's no big deal," Ivy said.

"You forget, I was born in the sixteenth century. Women were considered far too delicate to read such works, let alone be able to comprehend them."

Ivy made a sour look. "What a crock of shit."

"Absolutely, but nonetheless, that's the way things were. I was a delicate little flower who needed the protection of a man to survive. Women were in a far different place than where you are in this world."

"Again, I repeat," Ivy said tartly, "a crock of shit."

"Back to focus here, folks." Colin was staring out the door through narrowed eyes.

He was right. There was no time to go down memory lane. Right now Meriel was beyond pissed off.

Riah cocked her head and, for a moment, closed her eyes. The air changed and a scent she remembered well floated in the air. It was faint and the others wouldn't catch it. It made her shudder.

"Movement," Colin whispered.

For the second time, she drew her sword. She motioned for Ivy and Adriana to take their places. She and Colin had finally persuaded them to at least stand back. They could serve as the second line of defense, but the first line belonged to the two who knew the game best. Ivy and Adriana held wooden stakes, and Riah hoped to God neither of them would need to use them.

Even though the sword felt natural in her hands, it had been a very long time since she had been in the fight. Her entire body buzzed as if electrically charged. Did it always? She couldn't seem to remember. Or maybe it was because the scent of Meriel shoved every other rational thought out of her head. It was like catnip, and she wanted to roll around in it until her entire body was covered with Meriel's scent.

She readied herself for battle and pushed aside thoughts of Meriel. The creature coming for her now was no longer her fresh-faced lover. Outside her door crept a bloodthirsty and vengeful Destiny. She might very well look like her lover, but she wasn't even close. Destiny was a vampire, an immortal, and a murderer.

The door swung in slowly, almost slow-motion. Finally, Riah could see a hand, then a leg, then a face. For the first time in five centuries, Riah gazed upon the face of the woman she'd loved with all her heart. A shot of electricity surged through her as she looked into Meriel's green eyes.

Then it hit her. It was all in the past tense. It didn't have a thing to do with believing Meriel died all those years ago. No, it was past tense because that's where the relationship belonged—in the past. Yes, she'd once loved Meriel. In another time and place, when she was another person.

Though Riah knew she looked as young as she had on the night of that fateful party, over the years, she'd grown up. The love she'd felt for Meriel was first love, and though it would always hold a special place in her heart, it wasn't the forever kind of love. What she felt for Adriana was, and Riah realized it just in time to take the knowledge to her grave.

Riah glanced back at Adriana and their eyes met. She'd swear Adriana could read her mind, and the expression that passed over her lover's face made her heart flip. Why couldn't she have figured this out before tonight?

Quiet laughter filled the room and Riah snapped her gaze back to her former lover. "Meriel." She willed her hands not to shake.

Meriel raised a perfect eyebrow and her green eyes glittered under the harsh fluorescent lights. "I prefer Destiny. Meriel died a long time ago. I'm sure you remember."

"I thought you were dead." She was surprised that saying the words out loud didn't hurt as much as she'd have believed.

"Didn't take the time to find out, now did you, Catherine?"

Guilt wouldn't work. "It doesn't matter now."

"It doesn't matter?" Meriel's voice rose. "Do you have any idea what it's like to be left for dead only to discover you're not? I was alone, Catherine, alone and undead. I had no idea what was happening to me and was left behind to figure it out. No Rodolphe holding my hand and taking me down the merry undead path. I hid for months, then years, taking blood from anyone or anything just to survive. I was like a feral cat while you lived like a queen."

The bitterness in Meriel's voice cut right through her. She'd have done anything to keep Meriel at her side years ago, but she couldn't possibly convince her of that now. It was too late to make amends.

"I hardly lived like a queen," Riah said, defending herself as best she could.

"Different ideas of a queen, baby."

Riah ignored the taunt. "What do you want, Meriel?"

"I said my name is Destiny."

Riah was growing tired of the game. "Fine. What the fuck do you want, *Destiny*?"

Meriel's voice was almost a purr. "I want you dead."

Big fucking surprise. She and Colin had already dispatched the two guard dogs Meriel sent in, but there were more. Riah could smell them. Despite the fact Meriel brazenly walked into the room alone, she was far from it. The woman Riah had known never went anywhere alone. She needed people. Somewhere close by, her reinforcements waited for a signal. Riah hoped she and Colin would pick up on it before the others charged.

Out of the corner of her eye she noticed Colin tense. It had to be hard for him to push aside all of his training. To not swing and take Meriel's head right now, he must be calling upon every ounce of self-control he possessed.

They didn't dare make such a bold move yet. Meriel would be expecting it. Patience was one of the few weapons they had at their disposal and the one most powerful at the moment.

Meriel cut her gaze over to Colin. "Tsk, tsk, little man. I could snap your neck like a dried chicken bone, so stand down."

Colin didn't move.

Meriel tilted her head and studied him closer. Her eyes narrowed and she licked her lips. "I'll take you down so you'll never see it coming."

"Step back," Riah told Colin, without turning her gaze from Meriel's face.

She didn't trust Meriel and she needed him alive and kicking… or, rather, swinging. He better be handy with that sword. All of their lives might depend on it.

"That's a good boy," Meriel purred. "Now, where were we? Oh, yes, me alone, sucking on pigs and cows and filthy beggars so I could survive. All so one day, I could kick your ass. I think—" Meriel smiled large, her fangs long and white, "—that day is today."

This time, Riah smiled, her own fangs menacing. "Bring it on, bitch."

Chapter Twenty-one

Everything happened in a blur. One minute they were talking, and the next, a whirlwind as powerful as a tornado tearing through a small town hit them. Ivy felt as though the breath was being sucked from her lungs, leaving her paper-doll flat.

Colin spun when a flash of movement came from his left side, while Riah and the other vampire barreled straight for each other. Three vampires had burst through the door just about the time Riah swung her sword. Two headed straight for Colin, while the third joined in against Riah.

One of the young vampires, a woman, screamed, and Ivy glanced to her side in time to see Adriana fly against the back wall. She struck the concrete wall with a terrible thud and slid limply to the floor. The stake she'd held skidded across the floor and stopped when it hit the body of the dead security guard. Ivy dropped her own stake and crawled as fast as she could, keeping low to the ground.

Ivy put her ear close to Adriana's lips and listened. In the cacophony of sound and movement, she couldn't hear a thing. *Let her be alive.*

She pressed two fingers to Adriana's neck, grateful when she felt a strong pulse. *Thank God.* She returned her attention to the battle, pleased that no one seemed to be paying much attention to her.

Despite each being outnumbered two to one, Colin and Riah were standing their ground. Any relief that knowledge gave her didn't last long. Even as strong as they were, they couldn't hold off the powerful attackers for long. Sheer numbers were against them. Ivy had to do something.

In a quick sweep, she scanned the room. Her discarded stake was too close to the fighting and she couldn't reach it without jeopardizing both herself and Colin. Pushed against the bank of drawers on the far wall, she spied Riah's big black bag.

Keeping low, with her back to the wall, Ivy skirted the kicks, swings, and roars until she reached the bag. Groping inside, she touched thick wooden stakes. She gripped one firmly and pulled it free, then grabbed a second and tucked it into the back of her jeans.

Once more she began to inch forward, except this time instead of moving around the perimeter of the room, she inched toward the fray. She waited as bodies whirled and swords clashed. Finally, her chance came. A female vampire, in skin-tight blue jeans and a revealing top, stumbled and pitched forward. Ivy didn't hesitate. She sprang out of her crouch, stake held high, and plunged it into the vampire's back. An unearthly roar filled the room as she arched backward, which was exactly what Ivy hoped she'd do.

"Colin," she screamed, as she scooted toward the wall and out of the line of fire.

He spun and in an instant seemed to size up the situation. Without so much as a pause, he swung his sword in a wide arch. A look of fury was etched forever on the vampire's face as her severed head flew across the room.

One down, three to go.

Colin's gaze connected with hers and he gave a brief nod. He got it. The surprise element was still on their side, but only for a moment. The second woman fighting in tandem with the now-unmoving corpse hissed and flew directly toward Ivy. The sight of her rage-contorted face coming at her made Ivy back up even farther. Luckily she had enough foresight to pull the second stake from the back of her jeans and hold it straight out in front of her with both hands. The angle was perfect. She braced her back against the wall, both hands on the stake. The vampire struck, the momentum forcing the stake into its heart, but victory lasted only a moment.

Too late Ivy realized that not only had the stake penetrated the heart of the vampire but pierced her own body as well.

"No!" Colin's scream echoed in her ears a second before everything went black.

❖

Ivy went down, a spreading stain of bright red in the middle of her shirt. Colin didn't pause as he swung his sword at the vampire impaled on the same stake piercing Ivy's mid-section. With a whoosh, the vampire's head tumbled to the floor. Blood flew in all directions, hitting him in the face and leaving streaks of crimson across the floors and the wall.

He knew Riah needed help with Destiny and another male. Yet he didn't move toward her. Instead, he fell to his knees next to Ivy and slid in the blood on the floor.

She had her hands pressed against her stomach, and he covered them with his. A river of crimson flowed between her fingers and his broad palm, spilling to the floor as though it was an open faucet. Her face was white and panic rose in his chest.

"Help her," Ivy whispered, her voice thin and reedy. "Stop the bitch."

Colin didn't let up on the pressure. He had to stop the bleeding. "I'll get you to a hospital."

"No time." Her words were even softer now. "Stop them. Please."

"You're more important." Didn't she see? One human life was worth a dozen vampires, even a good one, like Riah.

Before now, he'd never have classified any vampire as good. They were unholy creatures that never should have been allowed to walk the earth. Ambassadors of evil and nothing more, they didn't deserve to exist. All hunters had lived by that creed for hundreds, even thousands of years.

Until now. Had he not seen it with his own eyes, he'd never have believed it. Riah Preston—or should he call her Catherine Tudor— was a contradiction. She wasn't unholy, she wasn't evil, and she certainly didn't seem to be an ambassador of evil. She didn't walk a path allowing her to be involved with the travelers of darkness or the human race. She fell somewhere strangely in between.

Even given her noble intentions, in this crisis moment, he determined valuc by the simplest of terms: human or vampire. When the life of the human who captured his heart was at stake, the decision was beyond simple.

He wasn't leaving Ivy's side. If Riah died, so be it. He focused all his efforts on saving Ivy's life. Riah would have to take care of herself.

"Stay with me, love," he said gently.

Her dark eyes grew hooded. "My timing always did stink." Ivy's lips turned up in a tiny smile.

"No, baby, your timing is great. I'll get you out of here and some good doc will have you fixed up in no time." He kissed the top of her head.

"I'm glad…" Ivy didn't finish.

❖

It sounded as though an army had just arrived. A roar filled the room. At first Riah was confused. What just happened? Then she realized what it was—Colin. He rushed into the battle, his sword flying so fast it was no more than a blur of red and silver. He screamed, though Riah couldn't make out the words. She could make out the emotion: fury. Meriel threatened the circles of hell earlier, but they hadn't made an appearance until right now, and Colin brought them.

She didn't have time to consider why. Keeping the two vampires at bay took every ounce of effort she had. Certainly she was powerful, always had been, but keeping two equally powerful vampires on the run was a problem. Actually, it was more like one equally powerful vampire and one getting up to speed pretty damn quick.

She welcomed the addition of Colin in her corner. He didn't seem to need direction and went immediately to the youngster, which left Riah and Meriel face-to-face.

Meriel smiled as she shifted just out of the range of Riah's sword. "Catch me if you can, beautiful," she purred.

"Don't worry, I plan to send you straight to hell," Riah snapped.

"You mean back to hell." The bitterness in Meriel's words cut, all trace of gentleness or taunting gone. "You left me there a long time ago."

"I didn't know." Riah jumped as Meriel tried to hit her with a roundhouse kick.

"Didn't take the time to find out either, did you?"

"I was nineteen years old. What did you expect?"

"You said you loved me." Meriel swung through another kick that just skimmed Riah's cheek.

"I did." Riah spun, holding her sword steady. She missed Meriel's neck by mere inches.

Meriel laughed. "Do you think I've learned nothing in the last five centuries? You can't destroy me. You're too soft. You walked away from the life and now you're no better than these humans."

Was that true? Riah had spent the better part of the last two hundred years finding ways to save lives, not take them. Neither human nor vampires lives. Instead, she'd spent eons trying to find a way to end her existence as a vampire so she might become mortal again. Perhaps Meriel was right, perhaps she had become soft.

Maybe she should give it up and allow herself to find the peace Rodolphe stole from her. To leave behind the endless existence might be the better road. She dropped her hands, the tip of the sword making a loud ping against the tile floor.

Then she saw Adriana. Her beautiful Adriana, who filled her heart with joy and might very well have found a way back to the living for her. Now, she lay in a crumpled heap on the cold tile floor and Riah didn't know if she was alive or dead.

"No," she screamed, and brought her sword back up. Rage infused her with power and determination.

But in that moment of uncertainty, she lost her advantage. Meriel was quick and deadly. Riah heard the swish and felt the breeze as Meriel's sword flew toward her neck.

CHAPTER TWENTY-TWO

It seemed to Colin, everything happened in a dreamlike sequence. One second he was holding onto Ivy, telling her it would be all right, and the next she was dead. Afterward, everything became a huge blur.

Without realizing he'd even moved away from Ivy, he was in the middle of the fight between Riah and the two vampires. He took on the man first. The young vampire was no match for him, when he was filled with righteous fury. It was bad enough this group of bloodsuckers had killed a good, kind woman, but throw in the fact that Colin loved this particular woman and fury didn't even begin to describe how he felt.

He'd give the guy credit, he managed to put up a pretty fair fight. Not good enough though. Colin only had to take a couple of swings before he sent the guy's head flying across the room.

He had just enough time to assess the situation before he had to act again. Riah lowered her sword, which surprised him. He'd sensed all along Riah was a warrior on a mission similar to his own. That she'd back down to Destiny, who was obviously evil, disturbed him. At least until the fire came back in to Riah's eyes. However, the fire was a hair too late.

But not for him. With a powerful swing, he brought his sword around and connected with Destiny's smooth white neck at the same moment her sword touched Riah's.

The impact of flesh and bone against his weapon vibrated all the way from his wrists to his shoulders. He powered through and heaved a sigh of relief when he heard, for the fourth time, the telltale thump. For a moment afterward nothing but silence existed. Then, it occurred to him, he'd heard only one thump. He managed to focus enough to see Riah still standing, one hand to her neck—the same neck that still had her head attached to it.

His sword clattered to the ground. "She's dead," he said to Riah, who looked as shell-shocked as he felt.

Riah stared at Ivy's body, then back at him, and darkness filled her eyes. Her hand fell away from her neck and Colin noticed that the wound caused by Destiny's weapon was superficial and already beginning to close.

Both of them turned when they heard a sound. Adriana, looking dazed and shaky, managed to push up to a sitting position. She looked around and shook her head. "This isn't good," she said at last.

Riah went to her side and gathered her in her arms. "Ivy's dead," she cried against Adriana's hair.

Adriana's eyes seemed to clear and she cocked her head. "Can you turn her?"

Colin and Riah said in unison, "What?"

"Turn her. Make her a vampire. Bring her back from the dead." Adriana's voice was strong and clear, as if being thrown against a wall and knocked unconscious was no big thing.

Colin started to say never and stopped himself. He went to where Ivy slumped against the wall and gathered her into his arms. She was still warm, as if she was just taking a little nap. Granted, she was wet and bloody, but he could almost believe she simply slept.

He brushed the hair from her face and wondered if he could still love her if she became the thing he hunted. It didn't take very long to decide.

"Please." He looked up to Riah. "Please."

"I can't." Riah stepped away from Adriana and stood very straight, her hands clenched at her sides.

"You can," Adriana said softly.

"I made a promise." Riah stood stiffly.

"And it was a good promise." Adriana moved to take both of Riah's hands. "But now you have to help a friend."

"I can't," she whispered.

"I helped you," Colin said, as he stared her straight in the eye. "You owe me."

"He's right." Adriana coaxed her. "He could have let you die and he didn't."

"You're sure?" She sounded hesitant and her body had relaxed a touch.

Colin looked down into Ivy's beautiful face. He'd never been more certain of anything in his life. "Yes."

EPILOGUE

Riah stood in her elegant bedroom and smiled. Funny how things changed. For half a millennia, she'd grieved for a lover she believed was her one true love. But she was wrong. She didn't feel love for Meriel, but guilt. Yes, she still harbored guilt for not checking on Meriel as she lay bloodied in the rain, for leaving her for dead alongside the road. However, the young made horrible mistakes then as they did today. It was just the way of life…and undeath.

Witnessing the utter lack of humanity in a once-tender woman such as Meriel was the wake-up call Riah needed. Oh, it was a few centuries late, but the old truism, better late than never, had some merit.

She turned and gazed at the painting over the fireplace, which made her smile more widely. The portrait she'd lugged from country to country, city to city, century after century, was gone. She didn't have the heart to destroy it. Not because she still had feelings for Meriel, but because she'd chosen to honor the artist whose name deserved to be remembered. He'd done nothing more than paint what he'd been asked to.

No, rather than destroy the work of art, Riah donated it to the National Gallery in Washington, DC. She didn't wish to gaze on Meriel's face ever again, and by putting it in a gallery far from home, she'd probably never have to. The folks at the National Gallery were delighted with her bequest, even though she stipulated that they never disclose her name as donor.

The murmur of voices pulled her thoughts away from the banished painting. Her guests had arrived. She tossed her robe aside and hurried to dress casually in cotton pants and a long silk blouse. A quick brush through her hair, and she was ready.

Six months had passed without a word, and as she neared the living room, she wondered if Ivy could forgive her. She hadn't wanted to do what Colin and Adriana asked of her. She'd wanted more than anything to hold to her convictions. She wasn't Rodolphe. She wasn't Meriel. She wasn't a monster. And only a monster would turn a beautiful human like Ivy into a creature of the darkness.

Then she'd looked at Ivy's still face and everything changed. As Colin held Ivy's lifeless body in his arms, she sliced her own arm open with a razor-sharp scalpel and let her blood drain into Ivy's mouth. At first, nothing happened, then, slowly, Ivy's chest began to rise and fall. The ugly wound in the middle of her body began to mend.

That was the last time she'd seen her. Colin had picked Ivy up and carried her from the room.

She and Adriana took care of the vampires and cleaned up the autopsy suite, after Riah made sure Ralph, the security manager, was alive and breathing. To keep him safe and out of the line of fire, she'd drugged him and tucked him into a locked closet for safekeeping. He slept through the battle as well as the cleanup. It was a long night but the gods smiled on them.

Adriana's house was a total loss, so it only made sense for her to move in with Riah. It was the practical thing to do, or so she rationalized—even though she knew better. She simply wanted Adriana with her, every day and every night. Not a day went by without marveling at her good fortune despite everything. Adriana was the real deal: heart-stopping, all-consuming love. Who would have guessed?

Also, Adriana had an amazing mind. Immediately after the excitement died down, she was back at work recreating the cure she'd come rushing to tell Riah about on the night of the attack. It might take some time, but, hey, time they had.

Now, Riah hesitated before stepping into the living room. Colin and Ivy stood close together, their backs to the door, while Adriana had one arm propped on the fireplace mantle. All three were sharing a laugh.

"Hey, you guys," Adriana announced. "Look who finally decided to show her skinny little ass." Her laugh filled the room.

Ivy turned. Riah's heart stopped as everything seemed to slow. Then, Ivy flew across the room to envelope Riah in a big hug.

"Thank you," she whispered with her lips against Riah's ear.

Her heart flipped. Could it be true? "You're not angry?" she asked hesitantly.

Ivy laughed and held her at arm's length. "Take a look at beefcake over there and tell me you'd be angry if you were given a second chance to jump his bones? I mean, seriously, Riah, would you pass that up?"

Colin shook his head and smiled. Love had softened the lines in his face. "Never thought I'd be the guy who'd find a vampire hot." He winked at Ivy.

Something dark and heavy fell away from Riah's shoulders. A weight she'd been carrying for six months. She crossed the room and put an arm around Adriana's shoulders, pulling her close and gazing into her amazing dark eyes. "I'm all about second chances."

About the Author

Sheri Lewis Wohl grew up in northeast Washington State and though she always thought she'd move away, never has. Despite traveling throughout the United States, Sheri always finds her way back home. And so she lives, plays, and writes amidst mountains, evergreens, and abundant wildlife. When not working the day job in federal finance, she writes stories that typically include a bit of the strange and unusual and always a touch of romance. She works to carve out time to run, swim, and bike so she can participate in local triathlons, her latest addiction.

Books Available from Bold Strokes Books

True Confessions by PJ Trebelhorn. Lynn Patrick finally has a chance with the only woman she's ever loved, her lifelong friend Jessica Greenfield, but Jessie is still tormented by an abusive past. (978-1-60282-216-0)

Jane Doe by Lisa Girolami. On a getaway trip to Las Vegas, Emily Carver gambles on a chance for true love and discovers that sometimes in order to find yourself, you have to start from scratch. (978-1-60282-217-7)

Blood Hunt by L.L. Raand. In the second Midnight Hunters Novel, Detective Jody Gates, heir to a powerful Vampire clan, forges an uneasy alliance with Sylvan, the wolf Were Alpha, to battle a shadow army of humans and rogue Weres, while fighting her growing hunger for a human reporter, Becca Land. (978-1-60282-505-5)

Loving Liz by Bobbi Marolt. When theater actor Marty Jamison turns diva and Liz Chandler walks out on her, Marty must confront a cheating lover from the past to understand why life is crumbling around her. (978-1-60282-210-8)

Kiss the Rain by Larkin Rose. How will successful fashion designer Eve Harris react when she discovers the new woman in her life, Jodi, and her secret fantasy phone date, Lexi, are one and the same? (978-1-60282-211-5)

Sarah, Son of God by Justine Saracen. In a story within a story within a story, a transgendered beauty takes us through Stonewall-rioting New York, Venice under the Inquisition, and Nero's Rome. (978-1-60282-212-2)

Sleeping Angel by Greg Herren. Eric Matthews survives a terrible car accident only to find out everyone in town thinks he's a murderer—and he has to clear his name even though he has no memories of what happened. (978-1-60282-214-6)

Dying to Live by Kim Baldwin & Xenia Alexiou. British socialite Zoe Anderson-Howe's pampered life is abruptly shattered when she's taken hostage by FARC guerrillas while on a business trip to Bogota and Elite Operative Fetch must rescue her to complete her own harrowing mission. (978-1-60282-200-9)

Indigo Moon by Gill McKnight. Hope Glassy and Godfrey Meyers are on a mercy mission to save their friend Isabelle after she is attacked by a rogue werewolf, but does Isabelle want to be saved from the sexy wolf who claimed her as a mate? (978-1-60282-201-6)

Parties in Congress by Colette Moody. Bijal Rao, Indian-American moderate Independent, gets the break of her career when she's hired to work on the congressional campaign of Janet Denton—until she meets the remarkably attractive and charismatic opponent, Colleen O'Bannon. (978-1-60282-202-3)

Black Fire: Gay African-American Erotica edited by Shane Allison. Best-selling African-American gay erotic authors create the stories of sex and desire modern readers crave. (978-1-60282-206-1)

The Collectors by Leslie Gowan. Laura owns what might be the world's most extensive collection of BDSM lesbian erotica, but that's as close as she's gotten to the world of her fantasies. Until, that is, her friend Adele introduces her to Adele's mistress Jeanne—art collector, heiress, and experienced dominant. With Jeanne's first command, Laura's life changes forever. (978-1-60282-208-5)

Breathless, edited by Radclyffe and Stacia Seaman. Bold Strokes Books romance authors give readers a glimpse into the lives of favorite couples celebrating special moments "after the honeymoon ends." Enjoy a new look at lesbians in love or revisit favorite characters from some of BSB's best-selling romances. (978-1-60282-207-8)

Breaker's Passion by Julie Cannon. Leaving a trail of broken hearts scattered across the Hawaiian Islands, surf instructor Colby Taylor is running full speed away from her selfish actions years earlier until she collides with Elizabeth Collins, a stuffy, judgmental college professor who changes everything. (978-1-60282-196-5)

Justifiable Risk by V.K. Powell. Work is the only thing that interests homicide detective Greer Ellis until internationally renowned journalist Eva Saldana comes to town looking for answers in her brother's death—then attraction threatens to override duty. (978-1-60282-197-2)

Nothing But the Truth by Carsen Taite. Sparks fly when two top-notch attorneys battle each other in the high-risk arena of the courtroom, but when a strange turn of events turns one of them from advocate to witness, prosecutor Ryan Foster and defense attorney Brett Logan join forces in their search for the truth. (978-1-60282-198-9)

Maye's Request by Clifford Henderson. When Brianna Bell promises her ailing mother she'll heal the rift between her "other two" parents, she discovers how little she knows about those closest to her and the impact family has on the fabric of our lives. (978-1-60282-199-6)

Chasing Love by Ronica Black. Adrian Edwards is looking for love—at girl bars, shady chat rooms, and women's sporting events—but love remains elusive until she looks closer to home. (978-1-60282-192-7)

Rum Spring by Yolanda Wallace. Rebecca Lapp is a devout follower of her Amish faith and a firm believer in the Ordnung, the set of rules that govern her life in the tiny Pennsylvania town she calls home. When she falls in love with a young "English" woman, however, the rules go out the window. (978-1-60282-193-4)

Indelible by Jove Belle. A single mother committed to shielding her son from the parade of transient relationships she endured as a child tries to resist the allure of a tattoo artist who already has a sometimes girlfriend. (978-1-60282-194-1)

The Straight Shooter by Paul Faraday. With the help of his good pals Beso Tangelo and Jorge Ramirez, Nate Dainty tackles the Case of the Missing Porn Star, none other than his latest heartthrob—Myles Long! (978-1-60282-195-8)

Head Trip by D.L. Line. Shelby Hutchinson, a young computer professional, can't wait to take a virtual trip. She soon learns that chasing spies through Cold War Europe might be a great adventure, but nothing is ever as easy as it seems—especially love. (978-1-60282-187-3)

Desire by Starlight by Radclyffe. The only thing that might possibly save romance author Jenna Hardy from dying of boredom during a summer of forced R&R is a dalliance with Gardner Davis, the local vet—even if Gard is as unimpressed with Jenna's charms as she appears to be with Jenna's fame. (978-1-60282-188-0)

River Walker by Cate Culpepper. Grady Wrenn, a cultural anthro-pologist, and Elena Montalvo, a spiritual healer, must find a way to end the River Walker's murderous vendetta—and overcome a maze of cultural barriers to find each other. (978-1-60282-189-7)

Blood Sacraments, edited by Todd Gregory. In these tales of the gay vampire, some of today's top erotic writers explore the duality of blood lust coupled with passion and sensuality. (978-1-60282-190-3)

Mesmerized by David-Matthew Barnes. Through her close friendship with Brodie and Lance, Serena Albright learns about the many forms of love and finds comfort for the grief and guilt she feels over the brutal death of her older brother, the victim of a hate crime. (978-1-60282-191-0)

Whatever Gods May Be by Sophia Kell Hagin. Army sniper Jamie Gwynmorgan expects to fight hard for her country and her future. What she never expects is to find love. (978-1-60282-183-5)

nevermore by Nell Stark and Trinity Tam. In this sequel to *everafter*, Vampire Valentine Darrow and Were Alexa Newland confront a mysterious disease that ravages the shifter population of New York City. (978-1-60282-184-2)

Playing the Player by Lea Santos. Grace Obregon is beautiful, vulnerable, and exactly the kind of woman Madeira Pacias usually avoids, but when Madeira rescues Grace from a traffic accident, escape is impossible. (978-1-60282-185-9)